Crack open all the books in

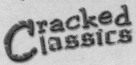

#1: Trapped in Transylvania
(*Dracula*)

#2: Mississippi River Blues
(*The Adventures of Tom Sawyer*)

Coming soon!

#3: What a Trip!
(*Around the World in Eighty Days*)

The Adventures of Tom Sawyer

Mississippi River Blues

By Tony Abbott

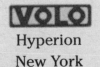

Hyperion

New York

Text copyright © 2002 by Tony Abbott
Cracked Classics, Volo, and the Volo colophon are trademarks of Disney Enterprises, Inc.

Printed in the United States of America
First Edition
1 3 5 7 9 10 8 6 4 2
This book is set in 11.5-pt. Cheltenham.

ISBN 0-7868-1325-3
Visit www.volobooks.com

Cracked Classics

Chapter 1

"Devin Bundy!"

No answer.

"Frankie Lang!"

No answer.

Well, no answer except maybe a stifled giggle.

You see, our English teacher, Mr. Wexler, was huffing down the halls of Palmdale Middle School looking for me and my best-friend-forever-even-though-she's-a-girl, Frankie (Francine) Lang. And by the growly tone of Mr. Wexler's voice—a tone we had definitely heard before—he was roaring mad.

"When I find you two, I'll . . ."

But he wouldn't find us. Frankie and I were hiding out in the janitor's tiny supply closet among the smelliest cleaning fluids and stalest work shirts that ever burned your nostrils.

It stank in there, but that's what made it the best hiding place. Nobody ever wanted to open that door. It could cause instant brain death to anyone who ever sniffed the air in there.

But brain death didn't bother Frankie and me.

"Wherever you are," Mr. Wexler said, "I hope you're studying for my test!"

"Studying?" I whispered to Frankie. "I don't think so. I studied for a test last year. I'm still getting over the shock to my system!"

"Tell me about it," Frankie said, nodding in agreement. "It was a one-way ticket to Headache City."

I had to laugh. I mean, everybody knows that Frankie and I aren't the best students in our class. In fact, we happen to know the best student in our class. He reads thick books all the time, and he wears pants so short you can see his socks.

"I'll find you-ou-ou!" Mr. Wexler said, finally. Then, rattling the lockers and pounding on the lavatory doors, he plodded away down the hall.

"Hurry, Dev," said Frankie, whipping a large square book out of her backpack and handing it to me. "We've got twelve minutes before Mr. Wexler tests us on this book. So crack it open and start reading. Unless you want to spend the rest of your life in summer school."

I shivered. "Summer . . . school. Two words that definitely don't go together! Okay, I'm reading."

I turned to the first page of the book.

On it was a picture of a smiling teddy bear wearing a cute sailor suit. He sat in a tiny boat in shallow water at the beach. "Are you sure this is the book Mr. Wexler is going to test us on?" I asked.

Frankie nodded. *"The Adventures of Timmy the Sailor.* He said it's a classic that he read five times as a kid. Now, read. We have to pass this test."

"One classic coming up," I said. I began to read.

Timmy the Sailor was in his boat.

Timmy was happy in his boat.

"Boats are fun, fun, fun!" said Timmy.

A sudden pain shot into my head. "So many words! The story's too complicated. I can't read anymore!"

Frankie sighed. "But, Devin, what about the test?"

"If we're not there, we can't take it," I said. "I suggest we just wait here until it's over. In the meantime, I've got a neat jumbo paper clip in my pocket. We could twist it into weird shapes. What do you have?"

It was cool how I won her over.

"Well, I've got some kite string. We can play miniature rodeo!"

"Frankie, you are the best!" I said. "Ya—hoo!"

But at the exact moment I shouted the "hoo" part of "yahoo," I flung my arms up in joy. This action dislodged one of the janitor's smelly work shirts from its hook. This is the reason no one sets foot, let alone other parts of themselves, in this closet. When the shirt fell from its hook, it settled directly onto my nose.

"Ackkkk!"

I accidentally breathed in the maximum amount of horrifying stink of the janitor's crusty armpit that it's possible for a human kid to breathe in.

"Ackkkkk!" I screamed again.

To keep the odor from burning my face, I ripped the shirt off and flung it away.

Right onto Frankie's nose. She let out a howl like a puppy whose paw had just been stepped on.

"EEEEOOOOOWWWW!"

She flung herself back against the door—*blam!* It suddenly opened, and hallway light flooded over us.

And a face was staring at us.

"Gotcha!" boomed the voice of Mr. Wexler.

We were caught.

Again.

"So!" said our teacher, a slow grin working its way across his face. "Devin Bundy and Francine Lang. Hiding out, eh? I should send you to the office right now."

A glimmer of hope stirred in my brain. We couldn't

take the test in the office. "You definitely should."

"But I won't," he stated. "Our test starts in nine minutes, and you are going to take it." Then he sighed. "Did you even bother to read the book?"

"We did read it!" I said. I held up the book proudly. "And I know what you're thinking."

He glanced at the book. "Oh, really?"

"You're thinking, how do kids who are so overwhelmed with activities—nachos, pizza, CDs, music, homework, pony rides, church, temple, school, shopping, sleeping, and, of course, more than four hundred cable stations—find time in their busy day to read a book?"

He stared at the book. "That's not what I'm thinking."

"Well, it's not easy," I went on. "True, we are completely swamped by life. Over*booked*, you might say."

"I wouldn't."

"But the reason we read this book, Mr. Wexler, is because Frankie and I . . . believe in books—"

"That's not the book I assigned," Mr. Wexler said.

My heart did a little fluttering thing. I tapped the cover of the book and spoke words. "*The Adventures of Timmy the Sailor*. It's what you said in class."

The man breathed out loudly through his nose. "Why would I assign a twelve-page picture book with a kindergarten reading level?"

Frankie shrugged. "To make it tough on us?"

"I did not ask you to read *The Adventures of Timmy the Sailor*," our teacher insisted. "I asked you to read *The Adventures of Tom Sawyer*! It's a three-hundred-page classic novel written by the great American author Mark Twain over a hundred and twenty-five years ago."

I looked at Frankie. She looked at me.

"Tom Sawyer?" she said.

"Yes," said the teacher.

"Not Timmy the Sailor?" I asked.

"No," said the teacher.

When he said that, my mind returned to its usual state. It went blank.

At this point, Mr. Wexler sucked in such a huge breath that if Frankie hadn't held on to me, I think I would have gotten sucked right up his nose.

"You—you—you—" he sputtered.

Frankie cringed. "We—we—we—what?"

"You are just not applying yourselves!" Mr. Wexler responded. "It's so—so—disappointing! If you two worked more—if you worked at all!—you really could become good students!"

Frankie jumped. "What a great idea. How about we take the test when we become good students?"

The teacher shook his head slowly, then pointed down the hall. "To class. Both of you. Now."

There was no reasoning with the guy. I had to act fast. I clutched my chest. "My heart is having appendicitis! Get me to the ER!"

I staggered down the hall to the front doors.

"Oh, no, you don't!" said Mr. Wexler, thrusting himself between me and freedom. "The only 'getting' you'll do is to be 'getting' to class, where—in eight minutes—you'll be taking my test on *Tom Sawyer!*"

"But we're not prepared!" cried Frankie.

"Be creative," the teacher said. "Stretch your minds. Dare I say it, think!"

Frankie scoffed. "Don't be ridiculous, Mr. Wexler. It's Devin and me you're talking to—"

He only grinned at that. "Come along, now. It's test time!"

Then, just when things looked darkest for us, there came a tremendous crashing sound from the end of the hallway.

Boom-da-boom!

And someone cried out.

"Help! Help me!"

Chapter 2

At the end of the hall was a walking pile of books. A huge pile. A teetering, wobbling, wiggling skyscraper of books! Not only that, but the books were sliding off the pile one by one, and one by one they crashed to the floor.

Boom-da-boom-boom!

"It's Mrs. Figglehopper!" cried Mr. Wexler. "Frankie, Devin, hurry and help her!"

We screeched over just as the last of the heavy books slammed to the floor. *Boom!*

"Oh, dear-dear-dear," said Mrs. Figglehopper, staring at the scattered books. "Dear-dear!"

Mrs. Figglehopper is our school's librarian. She always wears the sort of glasses that you look over or

8

under, but never actually look through. And she always—*always*—talks about books. I decided to beat her to it.

"You dropped your books," I said.

"It certainly seems I did!" she said, shaking her head.

"We'll help you restack your books, Mrs. Figglehopper," said Mr. Wexler, "then it's off to class for these two. We're having a test!"

"Oh, but Mr. Wexler, wait!" Mrs. Figglehopper said. "I think it's obvious I can't carry these books all by myself. Can you spare Frankie and Devin for a few minutes while they help me take these to the library?"

Our teacher arched his thick eyebrows. Then, glancing up at the clock on the wall, he grinned.

"Ordinarily, I wouldn't let these two out of my sight. But even a few seconds in a library will do them good. Maybe if they are near all those books, some of the ink will rub off. Ink? Rub off? Ha! That's a good one, don't you think?"

We didn't laugh. But Mr. Wexler did, all the way down the hall. Then, just as he rounded the corner, he said, "Please have them in their seats and taking my test in . . . oh! . . . seven minutes!"

"They'll be there!" the librarian said, smiling as she handed books to us. "Now, you two follow me."

With stacks of books in our arms we wormed our way through the various hallways to the school library.

"You know what I hate?" mumbled Frankie. "That we strained our brains on some book we didn't even have to read. How cruel is that?"

"Oh, flibbertigibbet!" said Mrs. Figglehopper, holding open the library doors for us. "Any reading is like exercise for you. Reading turns the light on in your mind."

"But what if your mind really wants to sleep?" Frankie asked, yawning.

"Then books can wake you up!" the library lady said. "And speaking of books—which I always do!—I think you'd enjoy the real story of Tom Sawyer much more than that little picture book you're holding. Reading classics is not as terrible or as difficult as you think."

I peered at Frankie beyond my pile of books. Because we've been friends forever, just one glance told me she felt as bad as I did. It was a bad, sad time for us.

Then we passed the clock on the wall over the checkout counter and we felt even sadder.

Our seven minutes had shrunk to six.

"I can't believe it!" said Frankie as Mrs. Figglehopper led us to the library workroom. "Just

10

taking a wild number, let's say there are a total of maybe five hundred books in the whole world. Okay, so how many do we actually have to read? I mean, how many good grades do we have to get? Shouldn't we leave some for other people? Sharing is good, right?"

"Frankie speaks true words," I added. "I say we already did the reading-a-book thing. Now we move on."

Mrs. Figglehopper chuckled as she opened the door to the workroom. "Oh, but there are thousands of good books in the world, and everyone can learn to have fun reading. All you have to do is open the book. It gets easier every time."

"Time?" said Frankie. "We have no time. We've only got five minutes to read that book!"

"Four, actually," the librarian said calmly. "But you can't read *Tom Sawyer* quickly. Oh, no, that's no good."

As we pushed into the workroom, my eyes instantly spotted an old broken set of library security gates standing against the back wall of the room. They looked like two sides of a doorway with no top.

"Zapper gates," Mrs. Figglehopper calls them. Busted, she says they are. Not true, say Frankie and I. Frankie and me. I. Me. Whatever. The point is, those zapper gates aren't exactly as busted as Mrs. Figglehopper says they are.

How do I know?

I know, because Frankie and I were in the library workroom once before. And we found out the extra-hard way that those gates can do something very weird.

And very impossible.

"Before you go, let me show you something," the librarian said. She pulled an old green book from one of the many shelves. "This is one of the very first copies ever published of the book you should have read. It's *The Adventures of Tom Sawyer* by Mark Twain."

"It's too thick," said Frankie, shaking her head sadly. "We never could have finished it, anyway."

"This book is over a hundred and twenty-five years old," the woman said. "And every bit as fresh now as the day it was written."

I sniffed. "Doesn't smell so fresh."

"True, and the covers are slightly cracked," said Mrs. Figglehopper. "But look here!" She opened the book gently and turned to the very last page. On it someone had written something in thick black ink.

"Hey, even I know not to scribble in books," I said.

Mrs. Figglehopper chuckled. "This is no ordinary scribble. It is the autograph of the author, Mark

Twain. Having Twain's autograph in the book makes this one of the most valuable in our whole collection. I consider it a priceless treasure!"

The phone at the front desk began to ring.

"Go ahead, read the first page," she said. "But be careful, some of the pages are loose. You have a few minutes before your test. Let me answer the phone, and then I'll be right back." She left the room, trotting for the front desk.

The moment I turned to the first page, Frankie raised her head. She was looking at the zapper gates.

Her expression told me that she was remembering the weird thing that had happened the last time we were in the library workroom. I remembered it, too.

It had happened a couple of weeks before, in this very room.

One minute, Frankie and I are fighting over a book; the next minute the book falls between the gates, and—*blammo!*—the gates go all fizzy and sparkly and there's this huge blue light and a weird crack opens in the wall—in the wall!—and of course we go into it and—*shazzam!*—we are not in the library anymore.

We are in the book.

In the book!

That's right. Somehow we got dropped right into

the story, with all the characters and everything! The worst part was that we couldn't escape the book until we read all the way to the last page.

Talk about brutal. Talk about exhausting. It's enough to make your head explode!

"Dev," Frankie whispered, still staring at the zapper gates. "I've been thinking. . . ."

I looked at the gates, too. "Well, stop it," I told her. "Thinking just gets kids like us into trouble. Besides, if you're thinking what I think you're thinking, you can think of something else."

"It worked once."

"Don't go there, Frankie!" I protested. "Okay, sure, maybe the gates worked once, but remember how we almost got totally deep-fried? I'd rather take a test."

Frankie chuckled. "That's not a line you say often."

"We're not going anywhere near the gates, Frankie."

"Okay."

"Because it'll probably turn out way bad."

"I said okay."

"All right, then," I said. "Because I have an even better plan! I saw a show once about a guy who could read a fat book in, like, two minutes. All he did was run his hand down the page, and his brain did the rest."

Frankie snorted. "Do you have his brain handy? Because I don't think yours will work the same."

"Do you have another way out of this?"

Frankie looked at the clock. She chewed her lip.

"I thought so." I began sliding my hand down the pages, flipping them over quickly as I went.

"Are you getting anything?" asked Frankie.

"A little," I said.

"So what's *The Adventures of Tom Sawyer* about?"

"There's a kid named Tom . . . and a closet and a wooden fence . . . there's a girl in here, too. . . ."

"This is not helping—" She reached for the book.

"Treasure . . . there's treasure!" I pulled it away.

"Give it to me!"

"You give it!"

"No, you!"

"Careful!"

"Oh, no!"

As if it were a basketball game and our fingers were straining to gain possession of the ball, we wrestled for the book. Then it happened. A page suddenly slid out of the book and fluttered across the room.

I gasped. "Oh, no! It's the scribble page! With the author's signature! It's valuable! It's priceless! We're dead meat if it gets torn!"

We tried to grab the page, but our hands

clutched only air. The page floated swiftly across the room, then took a nosedive like a bad paper airplane. It twirled in a wild tailspin right between the zapper gates near the back wall.

"Nooo!" Frankie shouted, leaping for the page.

KKKKK! The whole room went as bright as an exploding star. The next instant it was as dark as if someone had shoved a box over our heads. Suddenly, there was this huge crackling sound, and we saw the back wall—the wall just behind the zapper gates—crack right open.

Flickering blue light and wispy white smoke poured into the workroom.

"It's happening again!" I said.

Frankie's eyes were huge. "Boy, are you in trouble!"

"No, you!"

"No, *you!*"

"Frankie! Devin!" the librarian called out. "Time's up! Mr. Wexler wants you back in class!"

She started tramping back toward the workroom.

"Oh, man," I said. "We've got to get that page back!"

With pretty much no other thought in our heads, Frankie and I dived into the dark, smoking crack in the wall. We tumbled over and over until we hit something.

Something that said, "Hey! Get off my toe!"

Chapter 3

I blinked.

In the dim light I could see that Frankie and I were in our second closet of the day. Luckily, it wasn't a stinky one. But it wasn't empty, either. By the slim crack of light around the door, I could see a third person crouching in there with us, peering out. It seemed to be a boy.

I nudged Frankie. "Where are we?" I whispered. "And don't tell me we're in the book."

"We're in the book," she said, tapping the book's cover. "The zapper gates must have zapped us again."

"You're still on my toe!" whispered the boy. "Get off!"

"Sorry!" I said, jumping back next to Frankie.

The boy was about our age, dressed in rumpled jeans, a white shirt that had once been a lot whiter, and a tattered vest of brown flannel. Also, he was barefoot.

"Just for the record," asked Frankie, "who are you?"

"Hush!" said the boy. "My aunt Polly's just outside. She'll find us."

There was a scuffling sound outside the closet. "Tom!" cried a voice.

The boy chuckled softly. "Aunt Polly's all mad because she thinks I stole her fresh strawberry jam that took her so long to make. But I swear I never had a lick."

"Y-o-u-u—Tom!" cried the voice from outside.

"Tom's me," he whispered. "Tom Sawyer. I never saw you in my closet before."

"I'm Devin. This is Frankie," I said.

"Pleased to meet you," Tom said. Smiling, he stuck out his hand for me and Frankie to shake.

It was sticky.

"What's that stuff on your fingers?" asked Frankie.

"Jam," said Tom. "Now, shhh. We can sneak out if we're careful." Holding a finger to his lips, which he then took a moment to lick, Tom gently pushed open the closet door.

Thwack! A thin hand came down from nowhere and grabbed Tom by his vest and hung on tight.

"There!" snapped a voice. "I might have thought you were hiding in that closet! Out into the light with you!"

Tom, Frankie, and I tumbled out into what looked like a small, old-fashioned kitchen. Aunt Polly stood there, her feet planted on the floor. She was a thin, strong-looking, old-fashioned lady. She glanced at us over a pair of old-style spectacles perched on her nose, scowled harshly at Tom, and refused to let him go.

"Well, what have you been doing in there?" she snapped.

"Nothing," said Tom, wriggling in her grasp of steel.

"Nothing? Look at your hands. And your mouth. What is that?"

"I don't know, Aunt Polly," said Tom, his eyes wide with fake innocence.

"Well, I know what it is!" the woman said. "It's the jam I told you not to touch. So help me, I'll swat you!"

She reached for a stick that was leaning against the kitchen table—probably just for the purpose of swatting Tom—and held it over his head.

Suddenly, Tom pointed. "Look behind you, Aunt!" The old lady whirled around, and Tom shot out the back door like a rocket. He scrambled across the yard and leaped over a dirt-splattered fence and away.

"Why, you—Tom!" Aunt Polly called out. Then she grunted to herself, turned on her heels, pulled her glasses down, and looked over them at us.

"Well, and who are you two?" she said sharply.

Frankie gulped. "Um . . . we're . . ."

"New friends of Tom," I said. "Just passing through . . . your closet."

The woman shook her head as if it didn't matter, anyway. She took a deep breath and shook her head.

"Tom's played tricks on me so many times. But, my goodness, he's my own dead sister's boy, poor thing, and I somehow ain't got the heart to punish him. But punish him I must. I know he'll steal off and not go to school today. It's mighty hard to make him work tomorrow on Saturday, and, oh, he hates work more than he hates anything else, but if I don't punish him some, I'll be the ruination of the child. . . ."

Aunt Polly started mumbling to herself and got back to making more jam while we scrambled out the door just as Tom had done.

Leaping over the fence, we found ourselves on a dusty street in the center of a tiny village.

Out of breath, I turned to Frankie. "We're in the book, just like last time. I can't believe it's happening again."

"No kidding. It's the most impossible thing ever," she said, opening the book. "But it's worse this time. We lost Mrs. Figglehopper's precious scribble page. It's a treasure, she said, so we definitely have to find it. But where? It wasn't in the closet. Or in the kitchen, either."

"You know what?" I said. "I bet there's no way out of here without it. It's probably one of the weird rules of being dropped into books."

"Like when you try to jump ahead to the next chapter and the whole scene rips in half?"

I nodded. "Tell me about it. Everything cracks and we get totally toasted." I took a deep breath as we started to wander down the main street of the village. "I just hope we don't get trapped in this book forever," I said. "Things look pretty dull around here."

"Thanks for being so upbeat," said Frankie. "Next time I'll just lie down under the falling books."

As Mrs. Figglehopper had told us, the book was written about a hundred and twenty-five years ago, so that meant we were in the past. The village had a bunch of wooden buildings and houses on both sides of the street. The trees were heavy with leaves, the sun was shining, and it was fairly hot, so it was probably pretty near summer. Beyond the trees was the shore of a hugely wide river.

Frankie peeked in at the first few pages of the

book. "I think this small town is next to the Mississippi River," she said.

I laughed. Then I stopped. "Whoa, brain flash! I just realized something! This book is named after Tom Sawyer, right? Because the story is all about him, right? So all we have to do is follow Tom and we'll find the lost page!"

Frankie blinked. "Good brain flash. Where's Tom?"

We looked around. He wasn't anywhere.

"Maybe you'd better read some to find out," I said.

"Maybe *you'd* better."

"But you read faster!"

Frankie stared at me. "If I read faster, it's only because I always end up doing it more. Because you won't."

But she cracked open the chubby book, anyway, and did some reading, while I breathed in the summer air.

"Well, Tom gets into more trouble," she said after a few minutes. "He skips school, goes swimming, throws a clump of dirt at his little half brother, Sid, then wrestles a kid in fancy new clothes."

"Sounds like Tom knows how to waste a day like the best of us."

Frankie chuckled. "And for all that, Aunt Polly punishes him, just as she promised to."

"Brutal. Is he back in the closet?"

Frankie snickered. "No, he's got to do some kind of huge chore—"

"Chore!" I gasped. "Well, that's gotta slow the story down. Better read ahead to a more exciting part. Like the part where we find the lost page."

"I can't. The words are getting all blurry." Frankie showed me the book. All the words were hazy and impossible to read.

Ah, yes, the blurry factor.

We had learned from the first time we dropped into a book that the words always get blurry when you try to read ahead of where the story actually is.

"So we know one thing," I said. "We're right at the chore part of the story."

"Chores are tough news," said Frankie. "How about we go find Tom and cheer him up?"

"I'll tell him a joke," I said.

But when we found Tom, I wasn't sure he needed any cheering up. He was already pretty cheery.

In fact, he was whistling.

Chapter 4

Tom was standing before Aunt Polly's ultra-high, mega-long, and super-dirty fence with a giant bucket of white paint. He also had this long-handled brush, and he was whistling merrily like a flock of silly birds.

He'd whistle, then dip the brush, then whistle some more, then splash the white paint on the dirty fence, then whistle some more.

"He's way into the chore thing," said Frankie.

"Do you think all this sunshine got to him and he's gone soft in the head?" I replied.

"Palmdale has lots of sun," said Frankie. "And we're not soft in the head."

"Not too much," I said. "Let's talk to him."

"So," Frankie said to Tom, "Aunt Polly finally

nabbed you, huh? Big fence, little brush. Looks rough."

Tom slapped another brushful of paint on the fence and went on whistling as if he hadn't heard Frankie.

"Hey, Tom," I said. "Did you paint your ears closed?"

Finally Tom turned to us. "Oh, hey, Devin, Frankie. Sorry, I didn't notice you. I was all caught up in this."

"Take a break, man," I said. "Maybe you don't know it, but you're working!"

Tom dipped his brush again. He whistled a bit, then said, "Depends on what you call work."

"This is work," I said, tapping the fence. "Believe me, if it doesn't involve pillows and a remote, it's work."

"Not for me," said Tom, moving his brush a bit. "It's not every day a boy gets a chance to paint a fence."

Frankie and I looked at each other while Tom stepped back to survey his work as if he were some kind of artist. Slowly, he nodded as if it was good, then dipped the brush again and started on a new spot.

"Are you saying you *like* to do that?" I asked.

"It suits me just fine." Tom whistled a new tune now.

I watched him slap the dripping white paint on the wood and spread it around. He was making the dirty fence all nice and neat and fresh. It did look like fun.

Lots of fun, actually.

"Um, there's a lot of fence," I said. "Maybe you could use some help?"

Tom wrinkled his brow. "Oh, no, no. Aunt Polly's very particular about this fence. I'm the only one who's supposed to do it. Besides, you'll probably mess it up."

So, he wanted the whole thing for himself, did he?

"That doesn't seem so fair," I said.

"We've painted before," said Frankie, stepping closer to the bucket of paint and looking into it. "I mean, lots of stuff has paint on it where we come from."

"Lots," I said, stepping in front of Frankie.

"I don't know. . . ." said Tom.

"I'll be very careful," I said.

Tom chewed his lip, then started shaking his head slowly. "Aunt Polly said not to . . ."

"I'll let you play with . . . this paper clip!" I said, slipping my hand into my pocket and pulling out my jumbo paper clip. It gleamed in the sun.

Tom gave this no response.

"Okay, you can *keep* the paper clip!"

Finally, Tom breathed in, took the clip, and, frowning all over the place, handed the brush to me.

"Just a little, then. And please be careful!"

Ha! I was too clever for the kid.

I grabbed the brush and began dipping and sloshing it on the dirty fence. "Look at me, Frankie. I'm an artist!"

While I painted, Tom sat in the shade of a big oak tree that stood close by, dangling his legs, and, still whistling, he began to twist the paper clip into different shapes.

I hated taking turns with Frankie, but she gave Tom her wad of wound-up kite string, and Tom forced me to share the brush with her.

We were doing just fine, but the story messed it up for us. Suddenly, bunches of other kids came along and traded Tom all kinds of stuff to let them join the painting fun that Frankie and I had practically invented.

By afternoon, the fence was done, and in addition to the paper clip and the string, Tom had a nail, a piece of blue glass, a bit of chalk, a toy soldier, a couple of tadpoles, six firecrackers, a one-eyed kitten, a dog collar without the dog, a knife handle, four pieces of old orange peel, and a fairly well packed mud ball complete with a pouch to carry it around in.

It was when I saw Tom laughing to himself at the end of the day that I realized something.

"Frankie!" I gasped, pulling her aside. "I thought I was tricking Tom into letting me paint, when the whole time we were being had!"

"That's crazy talk," said Frankie.

"Nuh-uh," I insisted. "Tom suckered us—all of us—into doing his chore for him! He didn't do any work, plus he got a bunch of really cool stuff! Totally for free!"

Frankie's eyes bulged when she realized it, too. At first she was mad, then she began to laugh. "Devin, Tom is good. He's very good. And you know what he is?"

"A character in a book?"

"No. Well, yeah. But I mean that Tom is like the original slacker. Actually, he's the role model for people like you and me. Maybe we can pick up some tricks from him!"

I was grinning now, too. "Whoa, good brain flash, Frankie. They call this book a classic, but it's more like a training manual on how to goof off! If there have to be books, I suppose this is the good kind."

Suddenly Frankie had the same sort of twinkle I'd seen in Tom's eyes. "Actually, Tom has given me an idea. Let's get him to help us find the lost page. If we tell him it's treasure, I bet he'll help us!"

We sauntered over to Tom as he stood there scanning the finished fence. "Beautiful," he said. Then he turned to us. "I'm hungry. Let's go snatch a pie. You first."

"Sorry, Tom," said Frankie. "We need to go find something else."

"What else?" asked Tom.

"Oh, just something hidden," I said. "You probably wouldn't be interested."

Tom's eyes bulged. "Did you say . . . hidden?"

"It's very valuable," said Frankie. "It's probably the most valuable treasure there is, but we've got to find it alone. Sorry—" She started to turn away.

Tom jumped. "Wait! I'm mighty good at finding treasure that's been hid. I know all the places to look. Let me help!"

And he did help. But we ended up having to wait a couple of days. Aunt Polly wanted Tom to stick close to the house the rest of Saturday. And Sunday wasn't good because Tom was in church for most of it.

Finally, it was Monday morning and we were on the dusty street when Tom came running by.

"Late for school!" he said, flashing by us.

"Stop!" shouted Frankie.

Tom screeched to a stop. "What?"

"You promised to help us look for our treasure," Frankie reminded him. "And you're going to help us."

"But school," said Tom.

"But . . . treasure!" said Frankie.

You could see the poor kid was all torn up inside. Suddenly, he grinned and tossed his books to the ground. "All right, treasure!" he said. "But we need to find Huck first." He started straight off into the woods.

"What's a Huck?" I said, as we crawled over bushes.

"Huck ain't a thing," said Tom. "He's a who!"

"Huck's a who?" said Frankie. "Who is Huck?"

"Finn," said Tom, crouching under some low trees.

I gave Frankie a look. "I'm glad we cleared that up."

"Speaking of clearing up," she said. "Somebody should clear up these woods. It's a junk heap in here!"

She got that right. Just as we were coming around a twist in the path, we came upon a little area scattered with open cans and bottles, and featuring a smoldering fire and a pair of ragged pants hanging on a branch. And, oh yeah, an enormous barrel with two mud-caked feet sticking out of it.

Before I could say something funny, a voice echoed out of the barrel.

"Hey, you, get out of my yard!"

Chapter 5

We stood there, frozen to the spot, staring at the feet.

Suddenly, Tom gave out a yelping sort of laugh. "Everybody, meet Huckleberry Finn! Known as Huck to his friends."

"Except I don't have any friends," the voice in the barrel said. "And I like it pretty fine that way."

At that moment, Tom kicked the barrel over, and out rolled a kid in a rumply old coat, a filthy shirt, a crumpled top hat, and a very bad look about him.

Huckleberry Finn was maybe a year or two older than Tom, but he was dressed in what looked like the clothes of grown-ups. His coat hung nearly to his heels, and one skinny suspender held up his pants, which were so long they dragged behind him in the dirt and had been worn to fringes on the bottom. Everything sagged and dragged on him.

"Hey, Tom," he said. "Come on over to my yard. But watch your step so you don't smush my garden. It's looking good this year."

Huck's "garden" was a clump of saggy weeds, and his "yard" was nothing more than a dried-up swamp.

"Nice place you got here," said Frankie.

Huck snorted a laugh.

"It suits me just fine," he said. "Nobody likes me much, mainly because I don't do anything, don't listen to anyone, don't obey any rules, don't go to school or church, don't have money to pay for things, sleep when I want, stay up late, and live in a pickle barrel."

"I'm impressed," said Frankie.

"And I'm hungry," I said. "Do you have any actual pickles in there?"

"Got a dead cat," said Huck. He reached into the barrel and pulled out a string. To the end of the string was tied a furry stiff thing that might once have been a cat, but now looked more like the kind of hat grandmothers wear when they go to church. It smelled quite a bit.

Frankie sighed. "No treasure, huh?"

"This here cat's sort of a treasure," Huck said with a wide grin. "Traded a kid for him. Gave him a blue ticket and a bladder I got from the slaughterhouse."

"Dude," I said, backing away from the ripe smell. "I have to ask. Why do you keep a dead cat, instead of, say, the more normal pet, a live cat?"

"Dead ones smell more," said Tom, peering at it.

"I ought to know," said Huck. "I've been sleeping on it for three days now!"

"I don't sleep on dead cats," I said, "but sometimes I sleep with my CD player under my pillow!"

"What's a CD player?" asked Tom.

"What's a pillow? asked Huck.

"Excuse me," said Frankie. "This is fun, but let's not get sidetracked here. Huck, can you help us find some lost treasure?"

Huck laughed. "Forget treasure! Dead cats cure warts!" Then with one thumb still holding onto the cat, he hooked the other into his single suspender and breathed in deeply. "It's simple science, really. You take your dead cat to the graveyard at midnight where some wicked person is buried. When the evil spirits come for his soul, you heave your dead cat after them and say real loud, 'Spirit follow corpse, cat follow spirit, warts follow cat!' Poof! The warts are gone!"

Tom's eyes lit up. "I'm convinced! When do we go?"

"Tonight," said Huck. "I've got to plant some more

33

weeds. But after that I'm pretty free. Besides, I reckon the spirits will collect old Hoss Williams tonight. He was bad. He's been buried in his grave for a few days already."

"Nice," said Frankie, making a face. "Graveyards. Nighttime. Dead people. Not my favorite things. And what about the very valuable, one-of-kind, lost, and missing treasure we need to find?"

"Let's do the warts first," said Tom.

"No, I want to do the treasure," said Frankie.

"Warts," said Huck. "I got the dead cat and all."

"Treasure!" insisted Frankie.

"Warts!" said Tom, stomping his feet. "Warts, warts, warts! Besides, lots of treasure is buried in grave-yards."

I looked at Frankie. "Maybe Tom's got a point. There is all that digging, and those piles of loose dirt, and all those holes. The lost page has got to be some-where in the story. It might just be in the graveyard."

Frankie grumbled. "You're right, I guess," she said. "But I still hate it. If we do the warts now, can we do the treasure later?"

"It's a deal!" said Tom. "Huck, you come and meow outside my house tonight. We'll sneak out to meet you."

"Meow?" I said. "Just like what that dead cat will never do?"

Huck chuckled at that, then turned to Tom. "When do you reckon we should do this?"

"The usual time for such things," said Tom.

"Let me guess—midnight?" said Frankie.

"Midnight exactly!" Tom affirmed.

"Midnight in a graveyard with a dead cat," I said.

"A dead cat on a string!" Huck reminded us.

Suddenly, a distant bell rang, in a sort of shrieky tone.

Ding-ding-ding-ding!

"School bell," said Huck, laughing as he crawled back into his barrel. "Time to sleep. . . ."

But when Tom heard the bell, his eyes bugged out and he jumped a foot and a half. "Holy crow, I'm late! Mr. Dobbin will have my hide for sure!"

Without another word, Tom took off like a rocket.

And because this was *The Adventures of Tom Sawyer* and not *The Adventures of Sleeping Barrel Boy*, Frankie and I blasted off after him.

Chapter 6

Tom raced up the dusty road toward the school-house, but Frankie was a good runner and caught up to him.

Exhausted, Tom slowed down. "You run pretty good, Frankie. Sometimes I race Amy Lawrence, but she doesn't run so fast as you."

"Who's Amy Lawrence?" I asked, between huffs and puffs. "What is she, your girlfriend or something?"

I was just being funny, but as we crept quietly up to the schoolhouse Tom surprised me.

"We're what you call engaged, Amy and me," he said, matter-of-factly. "I've been sweet on her for about—"

He stopped dead. He stared through the window and into the room. Frankie and I peered in also.

There was a girl sitting in a seat near the window. She was not bad looking. She had on a blue dress and wore her blond hair wound into two long braids.

"Is that Amy Lawrence?" Frankie asked.

"Amy who?" Tom replied, his jaw going slack.

"Wait, you mean you don't know this girl?" I asked.

"I'd sure like to," said Tom. "She must be new."

I grinned. "Oh, I get it. The old *Love Boat* has floated up the Mississippi. Uh-huh, and it's docking right here!"

Frankie snarled. "Uck! Don't make me barf, Dev—"

"Oh, and look who's getting off the boat. It's Dr. Love himself! Tom, your problems are over. Dr. Love is here to give you love advice—"

"Devin, don't you dare!" said Frankie sharply. "If you mess up this story, there may be no way out of it!"

Suddenly, there was a rap on the window. And, in place of the pretty girl with braids, there was the face of a scowling teacher guy!

"Mr. Dobbin!" Tom gasped. "Let's get in there fast!"

But when we dashed into the schoolhouse, we nearly dashed right out again. The place was so small, the inside was almost outside. It was just one classroom with a roof. It had no computers, no over-head projector, no bookcases, no tissue boxes, and no lights. The kids were all crammed onto hard benches, the girls on one side and the boys on the other.

Frankie and I sneaked into the back of the room. Tom tried to, too, but he got caught.

The teacher swiveled on his heels and glared at Tom. "You won't get past me, Thomas Sawyer. So tell me: where have you been?"

I watched Tom's eyes drift around the room, then suddenly he twitched. I glanced where he was looking.

"The new girl!" I whispered, nudging Frankie.

Next to this girl was the only empty place in the room.

Tom looked straight at Mr. Dobbin and said, "I stopped to talk with Huckleberry Finn!"

"Ackkkk!" went Mr. Dobbin. "You . . . you did what?"

Still grinning, Tom repeated his sin.

"I stopped to talk with Huck Finn!"

Making a big sucking noise with his nostrils, Mr. Dobbin cried, "Huck Finn! That . . . that . . . well! I will deal with you later, Thomas Sawyer, but first, go—yes, go—and sit with the *girls*! I see a place next to Rebecca Thatcher. Go! And let this be a warning to you!"

Nudges and winks and whispers and giggles

rolled across the room, but Tom strode boldly over to the new girl and plopped himself right down next to her.

That's when I realized that Tom had pulled another scam. He had admitted that he'd visited Huck just so he'd be told to sit next to the new girl!

"Oooh, Dr. Love is in the building," I whispered.

"Gag me!" Frankie replied under her breath.

"Quiet back there!" shouted Mr. Dobbin.

I watched as Tom and Rebecca (Frankie told me that in the book she was mostly called Becky) Thatcher started to whisper to each other under the teacher's nose. Soon, they began passing notes back and forth.

As soon as I saw the notes, I thought of note paper. Then I thought of just regular paper. Then I thought of paper pages in a book. Then I thought of one particular missing page in a book.

"The scribble page might be here!" I whispered to Frankie. Like a detective, I squinted my eyes and looked around.

Frankie spotted the teacher fussing with some papers in his desk. "I'll check that desk at recess. Wait, they do have recess, don't they?"

They did, actually. A big recess. In fact, those lucky students only had school till noon! At the bell, they stampeded out the door and began to play.

While the other kids whooped and yelled loudly, Tom went to sit by himself on an old stone wall that surrounded the schoolyard. But he never took his eyes off Becky Thatcher. "Golly, I like her," he said to us.

I smiled. "Don't worry. I'm the Love Expert—"

"Kkkkk!" went Frankie, clutching her throat with both hands. "Choking! No air. Brain dying—"

I ignored her. "Listen, Tom," I said. "Here's how you meet girls. Let me tell you. My system is fool-proof."

"Yeah, foolproof," said Frankie, unchoking herself and glaring at me. "It proves you're a fool. Tom, don't listen to this guy."

I took the insult in stride. "Tom, everyone is amazed at my powers with girls."

"The power to make them sick," said Frankie.

"At least it's a power," I said. "Frankie, why don't you check the teacher's desk for that treasure we're looking for, while I help Tom with his love life."

Frankie gave me a look. Then she stormed back to the schoolhouse. "At least I don't have to watch!"

"Never mind what Frankie says," I told him. "Let me feed you lines. It never fails."

"Feed me lines?"

"Sure," I said. "I'll be crouching down below this wall and whisper great lines for you to say. Girls love

40

romantic goop. I see it all the time on TV. It never fails."

"What's TV?"

"Just something that never fails," I said. "Now, are you with me on this?"

He shrugged. "I guess."

While Tom sat on the wall, I squirreled myself down on the far side of it, just as Becky came waltzing over.

I was pretty sure she couldn't see or hear me, since the other kids were making lots of noise playing loud games in the yard. It was perfect.

Tom cleared his throat. "Ahem!" It was his signal to me to start feeding him lines.

"Nice day, isn't it, Becky?" I whispered.

"Nice day, isn't it, Becky?" repeated Tom.

"Mmm," she said. "It reminds me of one of those poems Mr. Dobbin read to us."

Ah! Poems! She wants the romantic goop! Even though the other kids were making so much noise, I came up with something good and goopy.

"Becky," I said.

"Becky," said Tom.

"You are like . . ."

"You are like . . ."

"A poem!" I said.

Some kid shrieked just as I said that.

"A worm?" said Tom.

"What!" said Becky sharply. "I'm like . . . a worm?"

"No, you're like a poem!" I repeated, as the kids yelled yet again.

"No, you're a live worm!" said Tom.

"Tom Sawyer! That's a hateful thing to say!" Becky cried. She stomped off a few feet and frowned at him.

I had to think fast. "Quick, Tom! Give her something. Girls like boys to give them stuff. It's on commercials all the time. And don't ask what commercials are—just give her something!"

Tom dug into his pockets and came up with my jumbo paper clip. "All I got is this!"

"That's good!" I said. "It's shiny. Girls like shiny things!"

"What?" said Tom loudly. "Girls are slimy things?"

"Slimy things?" said Becky, who had returned to give Tom a second chance. "So it's back to worms, is it?"

"No, please, Becky, take this . . . this . . . paper clip!"

She narrowed her eyes. "You idiot!" She threw the paper clip to the ground and ran off.

Tom growled at me, looked as if he wanted to kick me, then stomped off through the woods the other way.

"Good work, Dr. Love," said Frankie, coming up

behind me. Then she whacked me hard with the book.

It hurt. And when I opened my eyes, it was night-time.

Midnight, to be exact.

And Tom and Frankie and I were staring at that old dead cat again.

"Meow!" it said.

Chapter 7

Actually, it wasn't the cat who meowed. It was Huck.

"Meowww!" he repeated.

In a flash, we climbed through Tom's window and tumbled out next to Huck who was hiding in the bushes, grinning his sly grin again.

"Follow me, whoever's ready to say good-bye to warts forever!" he said.

"Mmm," said Frankie. "Nice invitation."

"That cat still dead?" asked Tom.

"Deader," Huck assured us. "Now, come on. It's nearly time." His smile was as wide as a jack-o'-lantern's as he darted off quickly and quietly toward the woods at the edge of the village.

At the end of half an hour, we were all wading

through the tall grass that sprouted up wildly between the tombstones.

The setting was the kind of graveyard you see in old-fashioned western movies. It was built on a hill, about a mile and a half from the village. It had a crazy wooden fence around it, which leaned inward in some places, and outward the rest of the places, but was upright nowhere at all.

Grass and weeds grew thickly all over the hill.

And, oh yeah, all the old graves were sunken in.

A faint wind moaned through the trees.

"That'll be the spirits of the dead," said Tom. "They're coming, and they don't like being disturbed by us."

Frankie snorted. "Well, we're even. Because I don't want to be disturbed by them!"

But Tom and Huck kept moving deeper into the cemetery. In a little while, we found a fresh heap of dirt, which meant that someone had been buried there recently.

"I really don't like this," I said.

"You don't like it!" Frankie grumbled under her breath. "I'm the one with the fear of dead stuff. And here I am, hanging out where the dead people live."

"It's Hoss Williams's grave," murmured Huck, creeping stealthily up to the dirt mound and sniffing it. He held his hand up so that none of us would come closer. I was grateful for that. Nearby the grave was a clump of three thick trees. Tom motioned for us to take our places behind them.

The spirits began to moan again at that point, and I have to say I began to sweat.

"I just had a thought," Frankie whispered to me.

"Did it hurt?"

"Sort of. My thought is, if the lost page is actually buried in that dead grave over there, you'll have to dig it up."

I made a scoffing noise. "Why should *I* do it?"

"The fifty-fifty rule," she said.

I frowned. "What fifty-fifty rule?"

"The one that says that when one of us thinks up an idea, the other one has to do it."

"I never heard of that rule."

"It's new."

"Shhhh!" hissed Huck. "The evil spirits are coming!"

A muffled sound of voices floated up from the far end of the graveyard.

"Who . . . or what . . . is it?" I whispered to Frankie. "What does the book say?"

Frankie's eyes were bugging out, trying to catch a ray of moonlight to read by. She shook her head. "I don't know. The words are too blurry to read! What if Huck is right? What if there really are evil spirits?"

"And what if they're coming—for us?" I added.

Some vague figures approached through the gloom, surrounded by an eerie glow that freckled the ground with little spangles of light.

Huck shuddered. "It's the spirits, sure enough! Three of them! Anybody know how to escape from evil spirits?"

"I thought *you* did!" said Tom.

"I thought *you* did!" said Huck.

"Oh, man!" said Frankie

"Here they come!" I said.

Chapter 8

As the spirits approached, I could see that the eerie glow that freckled the ground with little spangles of light was coming from an old-fashioned tin lantern.

"Um, do spirits carry lanterns?" I asked.

Frankie almost jumped for joy. "They're not spirits! They're . . . people! Three of them. . . ."

"And one of them is Muff Potter!" whispered Tom.

"Cute name," I said. "Not so cute guy."

Muff Potter was a large, sloppy-looking man who staggered out front, his arm out and his chubby fingers seeming to point to the grave. Two others were following him, but it wasn't easy to see what they looked like.

The cemetery, of course, was darker than dark.

"The second one is Doc Robinson," said Huck. "I can see his long coat."

Then, out of the shadows came the third member of the pack. It was a guy about seven feet tall, all muscles, and with a face that could stop a bus. Actually, it looked as if it had stopped a bus. The nose was all pushed to one side and the cheeks were bumpy and wide and the mouth was in a permanent angry sneer. He wore a hat pulled low over his brow, but the lamplight caught and flickered on his eyes, which were black and piercing and spooky beyond belief.

"Who's that?" I asked.

"Why, that's none other than Injun Joe!" said Tom.

A shiver went through me when he said that. I turned to Frankie. We were both thinking the same thing.

"Um, sorry, Tom," whispered Frankie. "Time out. We can't call the guy that name. First of all, it's *Indian*, not 'Injun,' and second, we would say Native American. I know that you're from a long time ago, but it's not nice to label someone with his ethnic heritage. It's insulting, and just plain inappropriate."

I nodded, big-time. "If that man is going to be a character in this story, we're really going to have to change his name."

"What should we call him?" whispered Huck.

"Well, he's tall," I said. "How about Tall Joe?"

Tom shrugged. "That's okay, I guess. But he's mostly mean and scary, not just tall. Plus, he smells awful because he never changes his clothes."

"How about Stinky Joe?" said Frankie.

"I like Stinky Joe," said Tom.

"Shhh," said Huck. "Look!"

We all went silent as we watched Muff Potter and the man now called Stinky Joe drive a wheelbarrow up to the fresh grave. In the barrow was a thick rope and a couple of shovels. The doctor put down the lantern at the head of the grave and came and sat down with his back against one of the trees we were hiding behind. He was so close I could almost touch him.

But he was fairly icky, so I didn't.

"What are they doing?" I whispered.

"Shopping," said Frankie. "But not for double-knit tops with three-quarter sleeves!"

Huck nodded. "Doc steals bodies for his experiments. To learn about what makes people tick."

"Or what made them stop ticking," Frankie added.

"Hurry, you two!" the doctor barked in a low voice. "The moon might come out any moment. We don't want to be seen by anyone. Dig. Dig!"

For a long time there was no noise but the grating sound of the two shovels slicing into the dirt and the dirt sliding off the blades. *Kroosh! Slup! Kroosh! Slup!*

50

Finally, one of the shovels struck the buried coffin with a dull sound.

"We got it," growled the deep voice of Stinky Joe.

Within a couple of minutes, Muffy and the Stinkman had pulled the wooden box out of the ground, opened it, and dumped the body out on the ground.

"He'll do," said the doctor. He wheeled the barrow over. The body was loaded into it, covered with a blanket and tied on with the rope. Muff Potter took out his knife and cut off the dangling end of the rope.

"Bring it to my house, and be quick about it," Doc Robinson said, but neither Potter nor Stinky Joe moved.

"Five dollars more," said Potter to the doctor.

"Right," said Joe, his stinkiness wafting over us. "And ten more dollars for me!" He clenched his fist above Doc as if he might pound him into the ground with it.

I was afraid. A glance at Frankie told me she felt the same way. I knew it was just a book, but the scene made me shiver all over. None of the three guys was good, but Stinky Joe was very, very, very bad. I could tell.

"Want more money, eh?" the doctor said. His eyes flitted around him once. Then he struck out suddenly with his fist.

"Take that!" he grunted. Stunned, Joe fell back.

"Don't you hit Joe!" said Potter, and the next moment he himself was grappling with the doctor across the little clearing around the grave. Stinky Joe sprang over and snatched up Muff Potter's knife and went creeping like a cat all around the tussling duo.

All at once, the doctor flung himself free, seized the wooden grave marker, and slapped it hard over Potter's head. *Ouch!* Potter collapsed to the ground groaning. That same instant, Joe leaped at the doctor, knife out. Then the doc fell silently across Potter, rolled off, breathed once or twice, then went completely still.

Doc Robinson was dead.

I nearly screamed and ran, but Frankie gripped my arm so tight, I couldn't move.

There was a rustling sound behind us and when Frankie and I looked around, Tom and Huck were turning away.

"Hey!" I whispered. "You're the main characters, you can't run away!"

"Try and stop us!" said Tom. He and Huck sped off into the dark, leaving Frankie and me alone.

"Our turn!" she whispered.

But then we heard a groan.

"Ohhh!" groaned Muff Potter.

I gulped a gulp that seemed to explode in my ears, but Stinky Joe didn't hear it. He just stood over the body of the doctor and over Muff's groaning hulk, considering. Then, taking the knife from his own hand, he slipped it into Muff's hand.

Three . . . four . . . five minutes passed before Potter began to stir more loudly. He found the knife in his hand, raised it, then let it fall with a shudder.

"Wha-wha-what happened?" said Muff.

"Something awful," said Stinky. "The doc is dead. Why did you do it?"

The moon went behind a cloud, but I couldn't make myself move.

"Me?" said Muff, quaking. "I never did it!"

"I saw you kill the doctor," said Joe. "I saw it!"

Frankie grabbed me. "That is so not true!"

"I know," I whispered.

"You two were scuffling," the Stinkmeister said to Muff. "Then he hit you with the headboard. You fell, then up you came, staggering, and took the knife and did it. I saw you."

Muff Potter's eyes were bulging with disbelief. "I . . . I . . . I didn't know what I was doing, then. It was all the drinking I did, I guess. It made a crazy man of me. Please, Joe, don't tell anyone what I did. Oh, it's terrible. You won't tell, will you, Joe?"

Joe shook his head, helping the chubby guy up. "You've always been fair and square with me, Muff Potter. I won't tell on you."

Potter began to cry, but the moonlight, coming out suddenly, struck Joe's face and showed he had no feelings at all.

I was totally creeped out to be so near the guy.

Muff Potter wandered off, reeling down the cemetery hill. Joe stood for a moment over the doctor, then strode off in another direction.

Frankie and I could hardly move. Shivering, I stared at the scene while Frankie stared at the book.

A few minutes later, the murdered man, the corpse in the wheelbarrow, and the open grave had disappeared, because Frankie had turned the page and we were gone.

Chapter 9

We found ourselves racing back to the village, too scared to talk. When we caught up with Tom and Huck, they weren't talking either. Their eyeballs were huge. Their skin was as pale as—as something really, really pale. They were stumbling and shaking.

Finally, I said. "We have to tell somebody."

Huck gasped in horror. "Us? What are you talking about? Suppose Joe didn't hang for the murder? He'd come after us like lightning. He'd end up killing us!"

Tom nodded his head, breathing hard as we ran. "But can we keep quiet about it? I mean, can all of us?"

We got to an old deserted building which looked scary enough, but was like the Happy Fun Place compared to the graveyard. All four of us tumbled in and fell exhausted into the shadows.

"Tom, we got to keep quiet about this," said Huck. "And to make sure we do, we'll sign a pact in blood. All of us."

Even in the shadows I could tell that Frankie got all stiff at the mention of that red stuff.

"Um . . . excuse me, but I've seen enough blood tonight. And I like keeping mine on the inside."

Tom nodded thoughtfully. "But a blood pact is the only way."

Frankie shook her head. "It's so unsanitary!"

Huck had already found stuff for Tom to write the oath with. On a loose shingle Tom scratched the following words:

Huck Finn and Tom Sawyer (and Devin and Frankie) swear they will keep mum about This and They wish They may Drop down dead in Their Tracks if They ever Tell, and Rot.

"Good words," said Huck, taking a pin to draw blood.

"Yeah, great words," said Frankie, "except for the 'Devin and Frankie' part. That part's gotta go." She crossed out our names, but Tom and Huck signed the bark with their blood.

Frankie, not wanting to see any more blood, hid her face in the book and started to read. Before we knew it, it was noon the next day, and Frankie and I were standing in the center of the village, watching the streets fill up with people. Every single one who passed by was talking about the same thing.

The body found in the graveyard.

"I saw Muff Potter washing himself in the Mississippi River this morning!" one man boasted.

"That's funny," someone added. "He never washes!"

"My nose can verify that!" the first one said.

"Washing is mighty suspicious after a murder," said a third person.

Frankie turned to me. "They've got it all wrong. I wish we could tell what we saw."

I nodded. "Me, too. But then—*kkkk!*—we'll probably have a total story meltdown. We'd better keep mum."

Pretty soon we realized that everyone was actually heading to the graveyard. I didn't want to go there, but that's where the book was going, so we had to follow.

It was creepy. The body of the doctor was still there, and now in the sunshine it looked even worse.

Tom wormed his way through the crowd to us. Next came Huck, pinching our arms and standing behind us. He was about to say something when a voice called out.

"It's him! Muff Potter! Don't let him get away!"

As the crowd turned, we saw Muff staggering back to the graveyard, wet and still in the same clothes as the night before.

Some men surrounded him before he could get away.

"Murderer," someone said.

"But I didn't do it, friends!" Muff sobbed. "Upon my honor, I never done it. Who accused me of this thing?"

The crowd separated, and there was the tall figure of Stinky Joe, standing there all silent and creepy, his eyes cold, his heart all made of stone.

"Oh, the rat!" Frankie growled under her breath.

The guy's steely eyes just stared at poor Muff. And he told the same lie he had told Muff.

"I saw him do it," said Joe. "He killed the doctor."

"We have to tell!" Frankie whispered to me.

I felt sick inside. "I agree this is all wrong. But we can't rewrite the book. We'll just have to hope for something right to turn this around."

Frankie grumbled deeply. "I hope this Mark Twain guy knows how to write a book properly. Muff is innocent!"

But no one else thought so. As soon as the doctor's body was taken away, so was Muff.

"It's not fair," Tom murmured.

"The jail is a cold place for anybody," said Huck.

"So how about we get Muff some food and things?" Frankie asked.

"Hey, stuff for Muff," I said. "Let's do it!"

Together, we managed to get a few things to Muff, sneaking up and passing him stuff through the window.

And just when Frankie and I hoped that something not so dark and murdery would come along, guess what?

Tom Sawyer woke up to a brand-new problem.

Chapter 10

Becky Thatcher was sick.

"She hasn't been to school in five days!" said Tom, bolting up in bed one morning, his eyes full of panic. "What if she dies? I won't be able to go on. I'll probably die, too!"

"Don't go off the deep end, Tom," I told him, as I crawled out from under his bed, where I'd been dozing.

"Right," said Frankie, sticking her thumb in the book. "If Becky dies, that would be two deaths in just a few pages. And a bunch of dead characters isn't good for any classic."

But Tom was grumpy and sad all morning.

Aunt Polly tried all kinds of painkilling medicines to cheer him up, but nothing worked.

He just kept mumbling, "Poor me, poor me . . ."

Finally, Aunt Polly booted him off to school to get better. As if school ever did that.

It was while we were trailing after Tom on the dusty road to the schoolhouse that Frankie turned to me.

"It's okay that Tom is worried about Becky," she said. "But I don't like that we're leaving the Muff story all hangy—and maybe Muff himself all hangy, too. You know what I mean?"

"I do know what you mean." I took the book from her and opened it to exactly where we were and read a few lines. "According to this, a few days have passed. It seems that Tom's not so interested in the Stinky Joe business now. I guess maybe it's sort of like gum. After a while the flavor fades and you need a new piece, you know?"

Frankie gave me a look. "Sort of."

"And," I said, "maybe we're getting a bunch of different stories about Tom. To show us what he's like. I mean, mostly, authors just give you one story and stick with it until it's done."

"Wait—mostly?" said Frankie, cracking a grin. "*Mostly* authors do that? Devin, how many books have you actually ever read?"

I counted on my fingers. "Including *Timmy the Sailor*? That would be . . . two."

"Case closed."

I jumped. "Case back open. Becky's back!"

It *was* Becky. She was playing outside the school-house as if she were fine and dandy and all better. Tom's moans turned to sighs, then to grins as he watched her from the road.

"Becky!" he whispered under his breath.

"Ka-ching!" I said. "It's appointment time for Dr. Love!"

Frankie grunted and tore the book away from me. "Let Tom figure out his own love life."

"Are you sure? Because I can schedule Tom in."

"I'm sure."

So I let Tom go out there adviceless. As bad as he did when I helped him, he did worse on his own.

There he was, pretending not to care that Becky had been sick or out of school or near death. He was doing the hard-to-get routine. And like him, it fell flat.

Becky stood there while Tom made loud war-whooping noises and jumped all around, snatched kids' caps and hurled them to the roof of the school-house, tackled a bunch of boys, knocking them all to the dust, and finally fell right under Becky's nose, almost sending her crashing to the ground.

The girl hopped out of the way, turned, and with her nose in the air, snarled, "Hmmf! Some people think they're mighty smart, always showing off! If I had that dumb old wire gadget you gave me, I would throw it at you all over again, Tom Sawyer!"

She stormed away, completely mad this time.

"Ouch," said Frankie. "That's gotta hurt."

Tom's cheeks burned. "Becky hates me!" he cried. "Everybody hates me! Aunt Polly hates me! Mr. Dobbin hates me! But mostly . . . Becky hates me!"

Frankie turned to me. "He's all with the gloomy."

"And the doomy," I added. "Sort of embarrassing."

But Tom kept wailing. "Oh! Everybody's going to be sorry when they find out what's become of me! I'll . . . I'll . . . become a pirate! That's right. I'll join forces with Joe Harper and Huck Finn and I'll live on an island! And I won't be part of this dumb world anymore. And I'll never, ever, never, ever come back!"

"But, Tom," I started.

"Ever!" he growled.

With that, he stormed away into the woods, just as the school bell rang.

I turned to Frankie. "Well, that didn't go so good."

"It could be worse than we think," she said. "We still haven't found the scribble page. And what if Tom bolts out of his own story? What if he doesn't want to go on as a character? Where will that leave us?"

"Stuck in the adventures of nobody?" I said.

"Exactly!" she said. "We'll be up the creek. It'll be

the worst thing that could happen. Worse than any-thing!"

"Or even worse!" I said.

"That's what I said!"

"Me, too!" I said.

We both gulped at the same time.

"We'd better find him!" I announced.

"We'd better!" said Frankie.

Together we ran into the woods. We hacked our way through that wilderness for what seemed like hours. Actually, it *was* hours. And along the way we managed to get lost three separate times. When we finally arrived at the spot described in the book, it was—as if you couldn't guess—midnight. Again!

The meeting spot, according to the book, was atop a small rocky bluff overlooking the wide, slow-moving river. It was quiet and peaceful there.

I breathed in the night air. "So, this is the big Mississippi River, eh?"

Frankie nodded. "The boys are planning to leave from here. I guess we're early."

"Who goes there?" came a sudden growl from the woods. We jumped.

"Um . . . just us," I said. "Who goes there?"

"Tom Sawyer, the Black Avenger of the Spanish Main!" said the first voice.

"And Huck Finn, the Red-handed!" said a second.

"Joe Harper, Terror of the Seas!" proclaimed a third.

"Name your own names!" boomed Tom.

"Frankie," said Frankie.

"Devin," said I.

There came a laugh from the woods, and the three boys broke through the bushes and stomped over to us.

"No, no," said Huck. "We're pirates now. Pirates always take scary new names for their new lives!"

Frankie chewed her lip for a while, then smiled. "Okay, for my pirate self . . . I'll be Sea Princess."

Tom spit out a chunk of ham he'd been nibbling, then started laughing. "Sea Princess? Pah!"

"Names must strike fear in others," said Joe Harper.

Frankie thought about that. "Okay, how about . . . Sea Princess of Death?"

"Better," said Tom. "Only change Sea to Creepy and Princess to Skeleton and I think you have something."

Frankie grinned. "Creepy Skeleton of Death? I like it!"

It was my turn. "And I'll be . . . the Horrible Doom of the Gloomy Night of Treachery's Fearful Screaming Skull of Death . . . the First!"

A rousing cheer went up. "We love it! Let's set sail for our island!"

"Wait a second, we're actually going to an island?" I said. "I don't like islands. Islands mean water. Water means wetness. I hate getting wet."

"But we got a ship!" said Huck. "Come on and see!"

The three boys tramped down to the water's edge.

I turned to Frankie. "How big is this ship?"

Frankie scanned the book. "It's not exactly a ship."

"Boat, then. How big is the boat?"

"It's not a boat, either," she said. "It's more like a, well, a raft."

"A raft!" I gulped. "A raft is like a large cracker that you sit on and hope you can keep sitting on until you're on dry land again! I don't like rafts! I really don't!"

A few minutes later, we were all crouched on a badly leaking bunch of boards that Huck called "the ship."

They had snitched it from someone's dock.

"It looks like a matzo," said Frankie. "Holes and all."

It sailed like one, too, with water splashing up through the planks and over the sides.

"Timmy the Sailor was very wrong about this," I grumbled. "Boats are the opposite of fun, fun, fun."

"Steady it is, sir!" yelled Joe, making our voyage sound even more official.

The raft drew beyond the middle of the river, and Tom and Huck "hit the oars," which were just planks of wood. Hardly a word was said during the next hour or so as the raft passed by the village. Two or three glimmering lights showed where everybody was sleeping peacefully.

The Black Avenger (Tom) stood still with folded arms, looking his last upon the town.

"I was happy there once," he proclaimed. "No more! I wish Becky Thatcher could see me now, on the wild sea, facing danger and death, going to my doom with a grin on my lips. Then she'd change her tune. . . ."

"To do that," I said, "all you have to do is—"

"Devin!" Frankie practically screamed. "Stuff it!"

I stuffed it.

The raft leaked plenty, but we soon plowed into the island and tumbled off onto mostly dry land. Our voyage had lasted almost two hours.

It was the middle of the night.

Tom and Huck dragged the mast and sail up onto land and made it part of the tent where we were going to spend the night.

Frankie looked at me. "Are we really going to do this? Sleep out here on this island?"

"The missing page might be hidden here," I said. "Plus we're all deathy and skeletony now, so who cares about bugs and snakes and cold weather and hunger and bugs, right?"

"Right," she said, gulping. "We're tough, right?"

"Very tough. Sort of."

That's Frankie and me.

Very tough, sort-of pirates.

Chapter 11

In less time than it takes for Mr. Wexler to pop a quiz, Huck fixed up a hammock more secure and comfortable than any you could get from an L.L.Bean catalog.

He grinned as he did the same for each of us.

"You know, Frankie," I said, "I'm deciding that Huck is one very cool dude. This hammock is first-rate."

"As long as it keeps me off the ground," she said.

Meanwhile, Tom and Joe were getting the first-ever official pirate fire going. We all jammed around it to warm the food and our hands.

I looked around. "Okay, we've sailed the pirate ship, we've landed on the island, what else do pirates do?"

Huck laughed. "Do? Well they . . . and they . . . plus there's . . . hey, I don't know. What *do* pirates do?"

Frankie raised her hand, since she had the book. "It actually says right here. Pirates attack ships, and burn them, get the money and bury it in awful places on their island where ghosts and spirits watch over it, and if they have spare time, they make people walk the plank."

"Good words," said Huck. "But I guess pirates do mostly bad things."

We all sat around the fire, thinking of all those bad things. Tom spoke unexpectedly. "I don't like that we snatched food from Aunt Polly," he said.

Huck made a noise in his throat, then wagged his head. "Or the raft we took. Maybe that wasn't right, either. Let's take a vow saying we won't steal again."

"We'll be the first pirates not to steal!" said Joe.

Everybody liked that idea.

Soon, all the other pirates and I, exhausted from our voyage and swinging more and more slowly in our customized, Huck-made hammocks, fell asleep.

When I woke up, I had nearly forgotten where I was. The early morning was cool and gray, and the woods were mostly quiet around us. It was so different from waking up to my noisy alarm clock at home.

Not a tree stirred over my hammock. Dewdrops hung on the leaves and in the grass below. The fire was out, but a thin blue wreath of smoke coiled up from the ashes and into the air. It was very peaceful. I liked it.

"Going swimming!" Tom yelped suddenly, and Huck and Joe bolted up with big grins. In a flash, all three pirate boys raced off to the water on the far side of the island where we wouldn't be seen by any villagers who might be out for a morning boat ride.

Frankie flipped out of her hammock. "Okay, Dev, if the page is here, we'd better hurry and look for it before we leave the island and this part of the story ends."

Together, we covered every inch of the island. There were hanging vines, clearings in the trees that burned from the hot sun right above us, and swampy areas where our shoes got stuck.

That was loads of fun.

Searching the place didn't take us very long, because the island wasn't that big. We didn't find a signed page from an old book, but we did see something else.

It was Frankie who spotted it first.

"A boat," she said, pointing to the river.

I peered out from behind the rock I was looking under. There was a little steam ferryboat about a mile below the village, drifting with the current. The deck was crowded with people. Then a big jet of white smoke burst from the ferryboat's side—*poom!*

It was a cannon, blasting a shot straight up the river.

"They're up to something," said Frankie.

"Hey, Tom!" I called. "Huck! Joe! Come here!"

The three boys came running out of the woods. They were dressed in leaves and branches and vines, fresh from playing jungle pirates.

"What are they doing out there?" Frankie asked. "They're firing over the water at nothing."

And as we watched—*poom! poom!*—the cannon started blasting again.

"I know!" exclaimed Tom. "Somebody's drowned!"

"That's it," said Huck. "They done that last summer when Bill Turner got drowned. They shoot a cannon over the water, and that makes the water roil all up and the drowned person comes floating up to the surface."

"Sounds scientific," I said.

"It's very," Huck agreed.

"I wonder who drowned," said Joe Harper.

Frankie thought about that, frowning for a while. Then her eyes grew big. "Wait a second! I know who's drowned!"

"Who?" asked Tom.

"It's us!" she cried.

Instantly, the three boys grinned.

"They think we've drowned!" yelped Huck.

"They'll cry now for sure. And us? We're heroes!"

Tom cheered and whooped for a while, then stopped. He had a strange look on his face. So did Joe, actually.

I had the book, but I didn't need to read it to know what was going on with the pirates. One look at Tom's face—and Joe's, too—and I knew they were thinking about people back home who probably weren't having much fun at the idea of the boys being dead.

Only Huck kept on grinning through every cannon blast. I knew that was because he had no family of his own.

"Maybe we should go back." Joe said.

"Never!" said Tom abruptly, probably trying to hide his own feelings. "That's just being chicken! Aren't you the Terror of the Seas, a great pirate who laughs at death?"

"Sure I am," Joe insisted. "I'm the biggest death-laugher ever. Ha . . . ha . . . ha . . . See?"

"Then that's that," said Tom. "Tomorrow, we search for treasure!"

After that, we all went back to camp and threw ourselves down, talking rough-and-tough pirate talk. But long before nightfall, the talk lost its rough-and-toughness. Tom and Joe went silent first. Then Huck.

They were sleeping.

When I looked over at Frankie, she was snoring softly with the book snuggled under her head as her pillow.

"Okay, then. Sleep for me, too," I murmured.

I closed my eyes and started to drift off, thinking about the pillows on my bed at home and how soft they were, when I heard a noise from around the campfire.

Popping my lids open, I saw Tom tiptoe off through the trees and break into a run in the direction of the river.

Chapter 12

I shifted into sneaky mode and followed Tom. Not only was I in the real dark but because Frankie had the book, I was in the dark about what was going to happen. Still, I figured that the story probably headed Tom's way, so I went.

He waded into the river and swam across at the narrowest point, not far from the village.

Of course, I got wet, too. I hated that.

Once ashore, Tom flew along from one alley to another, and pretty soon I caught sight of that very high, very long, very white fence Frankie and I had helped paint.

I chuckled to myself. "So, the Black Avenger isn't so tough, after all. He's gone home to visit his aunt Polly."

Tom edged over to the back door and slipped inside. I waited a minute, then did the same. Inside, he hid himself in the shadows, and I hid, watching him. There was talking coming from a lit room in the front of the house.

"He wasn't bad," Aunt Polly was saying, "only mischievous. He never meant any harm, and he was the best-hearted boy that ever . . . ever . . . was—"

I heard her begin to cry.

"It was the same with my Joe!" said Mrs. Harper. "Always full of devilment, but just as unselfish and kind as he could be."

She started to cry, too.

So did Tom. I guess seeing his aunt and Mrs. Harper break down was too much for him. He was about to crash into the room, when Mrs. Harper said something that made him stop.

"If the bodies are still missing by Sunday, we're going to have the funerals that morning."

Tom froze in the shadows while everybody wailed to think about funerals for their little boys, and even one for Huck, who was nobody's little boy.

Finally, Aunt Polly knelt down in the lamplight and prayed for Tom, and he pulled back into the shadows and went still.

After a while, Mrs. Harper went home, Aunt Polly went to bed, and the house was quiet. I saw Tom tiptoe into his aunt's room. He had a note all written out on a strip of bark. He took it out and reached over to her nightstand, but then he stopped, took it back, and gave his aunt a kiss. Then, just before he slid out, I slid out.

As he started away from the house, I jumped in front of him. "Why didn't you wake her up?" I asked.

"Devin?" he gasped. "What—did you follow me?"

"Yeah," I said. "And I think you should tell your poor Aunt Polly that you're alive. She was crying so hard!"

Tom's face was taken over by a frown. "I would have. Except for a secret thing I'm planning that's even better."

"What is it?" I asked.

"Never mind," said Tom. "And don't go telling Joe and Huck you saw me here. Go ahead, promise."

I backed up. "Whoa. Just don't make me sign anything in blood."

"I won't. Just don't tell."

I agreed, and we shook hands on it. Then we headed back to the island, which of course left me soaking wet again. It was morning by the time we strolled into the camp. Huck and Joe were showing Frankie how to make a slingshot from a thick tree branch and some vines. She was telling them about theme parks, but they weren't really getting it.

Huck and Joe and Frankie leaped up when they saw Tom, and explained that they were sick of the island and wanted to go home. Frankie was the loudest.

"We've done the island," she said. "Backward, forward, up, down, there's no treasure. We're running out of pages—I mean, time. So let's go back to town already."

But Tom insisted. "If we stay a few more days, something great will happen. Then, I promise, we'll leave."

Joe shrugged, then agreed. Huck agreed.

Frankie crossed her arms and grumbled to herself.

So we stayed on the island until Sunday when, in the early hours of the morning, we rafted back to shore.

When the five of us trudged down the dusty main street, the village seemed hushed and still.

At that moment, the church bell began to toll—*dong! dong! dong!*—and the streets began to fill with people dressed in their best and darkest clothes.

"What is this all about?" asked Joe.

Tom held such a big grin on his face, the corners of his mouth almost met in the back. "Funerals! For us! We'll be guests at our own deaths! That's my big surprise!"

Huck leaped in the air. "I love it!"

"Me, too!" said Tom. "Now, come on. Let's go hide near the church."

We scrambled up to the churchyard before anyone saw us and dived behind the bushes that lined the walk. The villagers headed into the churchyard, whispering as they trudged up the path, about the sad doings on the river, but went silent once they crossed the threshold and entered the church. Soon, the whole town was inside.

We crept to the door and peered in.

"I can't remember when the church was so full before," said Joe.

"I can't remember the last time I was in it," said Huck with a chuckle. "And now it's too late, because I'm dead."

"You're not actually dead," said Frankie.

"Oh, right," he said. "I keep forgetting."

Tom seemed to want to laugh, but his eyes caught sight of Aunt Polly and his half brother Sid and half sister Mary all in black. They sat next to the Harpers, who were also in completely black outfits.

"I almost want to cry for those poor kids," I said.

Frankie grunted. "Devin, we're not dead."

The preacher stood at the pulpit and began to speak.

It was a sorrowful speech. The minister talked

about Tom and Joe and even Huck. He remembered incidents in their lives that showed how sweet and generous they were, what noble and fine children they were.

The congregation became more and more moved as the minister went on, until at last the whole group broke down and wept in loud wails and sobs. Even the minister began crying in the pulpit.

"The time is right," said Tom. "And here we . . . go!"

With that, Tom pushed open the doors with a bang, and he and Huck and Joe strode in, all grins and smiles.

The minister raised his eyes from his soggy handkerchief and stood frozen in the pulpit. First one and then another pair of eyes followed the minister's, and then the whole congregation rose together and stared.

"The three dead boys!" someone whispered.

"They're marching up the aisle!"

"They're—alive!"

Aunt Polly, Mary, and the Harpers threw themselves on the boys and almost smothered them nearly to death with kisses and hugs and stuff.

The minister shouted at the top of his voice: "Sing! Sing the hymn, 'Praise God from Whom All Blessings Flow!' Sing, I say! And put your hearts into it!"

And everyone did. The sound was amazing. As if everyone had trained to be an opera singer, the sound of everybody singing somehow sounded really beautiful.

And while the song shook the rafters of the church, Tom turned to us and said, "What a day for us pirates! What a homecoming for a band of cut-throats!"

Becky Thatcher nearly hugged Tom herself. She settled for proclaiming that she would have a great picnic to celebrate the boys' homecoming.

"It's a great day," I said. "We're alive. Talk about fun, fun, fun? This is terrific!"

But Frankie pulled me aside and gave me a look.

"What's the matter?" I asked.

"Something we forgot about is coming back. Something not so great and fun."

She opened the book to the next chapter. I read the first line. I gasped.

"The murder trial of Muff Potter!"

Chapter 13

No sooner had everyone finished cheering about Tom and the boys being alive, than they started gossiping about the trial getting ready to start.

"It's all Muff Potter, Muff Potter, Muff Potter on the street," Huck said, when we met at the courthouse the next day.

Tom shook his head slowly. "I reckon he's a goner. I sure feel sorry for him sometimes."

"Muff's always been good to me," said Huck. "He gave me half a fish once when there wasn't enough for two. He loafs around, of course, but we all do that."

"I'm even an expert loafer myself," I said.

"He's mended kites for me," said Tom. "And helped me knot hooks on my fishing line."

Frankie frowned. "Maybe we could break him out?"

Tom and Huck both shook their heads.

"I heard people say that if he was to get free, they'd find him and hang him, anyway," said Huck.

That stopped conversation for a while.

"Let's go to him now," said Tom. "At least we can make him feel better."

That sounded good to all of us, so together we sneaked between the buildings until we were behind the jail. Tom went to the barred window and peeked in. "Muff?"

The balding head rose up slowly behind the bars, blinked, and grinned at us. A strange pain stung my throat and chest as I saw the poor guy in there. Like Frankie, I really wanted to bust him free, but the story didn't seem to want to go there.

Huck passed some tobacco and matches through the bars, and Muff looked as if he would cry at the kindness of it.

"You've been mighty good to me," Muff said. "Better than anybody else in town. And I won't forget it. Often I've said to myself, I used to mend all the boys' kites and things and show them where the good fishing was and befriend them when I could, and now they've all forgotten old Muff when he's in trouble, but Tom don't and Huck don't, they don't forget him! And I don't forget them! Well, boys, I've done an awful thing. I was drunk and crazy at the time, I guess, and now I've got to pay for it with my life. It's only right . . ."

We so wanted to tell Muff that he was innocent, but we settled for asking him if he had seen any lost page with a scribble on it in the jail. He shook his head. Finally, we all left the place, miserable and sad and feeling wrong about the whole thing.

"The author's not going to let this happen, is he?" Frankie said as we headed out to the main street.

"It looks like it," I said.

"But this is so wrong!" she said. "All the evidence will point to Muff being guilty. Everyone will be too afraid of Stinkhead Joe to say anything. He'll just be sitting there in the courtroom like some kind of . . ."

"Murderer?" I suggested.

"Exactly."

Tom frowned. "I'll meet you all inside the court-house. There's something I have to do first." He slipped through the gathering crowd and disap-peared.

After some minutes, Huck, Frankie, and I finally squeezed our way into the back row of the crowded courtroom, which was jammed wall to wall with townspeople. I looked around for Tom, but couldn't spot him.

Just as we sat down, Muff Potter was brought in, looking worse than ever. His eyes scanned the crowd, then he winced when he spotted Stinky Joe, sitting motionless in his seat, his eyes as steely and cold as ever.

"Poor Muff," I said.

When the judge called the first witness, it turned out to be that guy who had seen Muff washing. The man claimed that Muff never washed, so he must be guilty. The crowd murmured agreement with that.

When given the chance to ask the witness some questions, Muff Potter's lawyer said, "No questions."

The next witness was the guy who had found the knife near the doctor's body. Again, Muff's lawyer had no questions for him.

When the third witness identified the knife as Muff's, and Muff's lawyer still said, "No questions," I got mad. "Why isn't the doofus asking any questions?" I whispered to Frankie. "I've seen enough courtroom scenes on TV to know that you're supposed to make the witnesses seem wrong. Even I could do a better job."

"Devin, I don't think so—"

But I couldn't watch Muff take the rap for a crime he didn't commit. I leaped up, and pounded the desk of Muff's lawyer. "What kind of lawyer are you, anyway?"

"A trial lawyer," he said.

"Well, stop trying and do something!"

"I object, Your Honor."

"Did you hear that, Judge?" I said. "This man objects to your honor. How dare he! Fire him! Send him to jail! I'll take over the questioning now."

"But, you haven't tried any cases!" said the judge.

"I'll try anything once—*ooomph!*"

I was suddenly on the floor. Frankie had tackled me.

"Devin, you're spoiling everything. Muff's lawyer has a plan, and you're wrecking it, big-time!"

"A . . . plan?" I said.

Frankie nodded. "If you'd read, you'd know. Look."

Muff's lawyer stood before the court and said, "I wish to call . . . Thomas Sawyer to the stand!"

"Whoa! A little surprise here!" I mumbled.

Every eye fastened on Tom as he appeared at the side door. He took his place on the stand, looking scared.

"Tom Sawyer," said Muff's lawyer, "where were you on the seventeenth of June, at the hour of midnight?"

Tom opened his mouth, glanced at Stinky Joe's cold, hard face, and closed it again. A moment later, Tom seemed to get his strength back.

"In the graveyard," he said.

A crazy smile flitted across Joe's face.

"Were you anywhere near Hoss Williams's grave?"

"Yes, sir," Tom answered. "As near as I am to you."

"Was anyone with you?"

"Only a cat, sir," Tom said. "A dead one."

There was a ripple of laughter in the courtroom.

"Now, Tom," said the lawyer, "tell us what you saw when you and your dead cat were in the graveyard."

Tom began, slowly at first, but then more easily, to describe everything he had seen that night. He purposely left out that Frankie and me and Huck were there with him. To keep us out of all the trouble, I guess.

When Tom got to the big part, everyone in the room leaned in close and hung on every word he said.

"And as the doctor fetched the board around and Muff Potter fell, Joe jumped with Muff's knife and—"

CRASH!

As quick as lightning, the murderer sprang out of his seat, hurtled himself straight through a window, and was gone!

"Whoa!" I said. "Is that guy guilty or what?"

Chapter 14

Faster than you can say, "There he goes!" search parties of noisy men with sticks were combing every street and alley in the village for signs of Stinky Joe.

But nobody could find him anywhere.

Muff Potter was free, of course. But an even bigger thing was that Tom was a hero. The townsfolk carried him right out of that courthouse and down the main street, cheering and whooping up a storm.

Back at Aunt Polly's, Tom told us what he had done.

"After we saw Muff in jail, I felt so bad I went straight to Muff's lawyer and told him how I saw Stinky Joe do the murder."

"Good job," I said. "I was waiting for that lawyer to come up with something. It turned out to be something huge!"

"Tom, you sure made Muff happy," Huck added. "And Stinky Joe mad."

Frankie didn't say anything.

"What's the matter?" I asked her.

She pulled me aside. "Devin, I'm really glad Muff is free, but we're two thirds through the book, we've been to the school, the graveyard, the island, the courthouse, the jail, and no lost page. What if we don't find it?"

I grumbled at the thought. "Maybe it's hidden somewhere we haven't thought of."

Tom's eyes suddenly lit up. "Hidden? As in . . . buried?" Then he nearly exploded with the word.

"Treasure!"

Tom was already running for the door. "If you got something that's hidden, it's most likely buried. And what's buried is meant to be dug up!"

"I like the way your brain works, Tom," I said. "But where should we dig?"

"Treasure is mostly hid under the floors of a haunted house!" he said.

Frankie shuddered. "Haunted house?"

"Luckily, we got one real close," said Tom with a laugh. From Aunt Polly's doorway, he pointed up the street to a hill. "Over Cardiff's Hill. The hauntedest house in town. It's a real spooker!"

I looked at Frankie. Neither of us wanted to deal with a haunted house, but it was clear that we were running out of scenery in this story. We had to check it out.

"Point the way, Tom," I said.

So we picked up a couple of bent shovels and picks from the shed behind Aunt Polly's house and tramped up over the hill called Cardiff's Hill.

"There sure are a lot of hills back now," I said.

"And I think we tramped up every one," said Frankie.

"Yeah," I commented. "Who says we're lazy?"

A little while later, we stood by an old house. An old, *old* house.

"I see the guy who designed the graveyard also did this place," Frankie said with a snort.

I tried to laugh, but it was true.

The house was surrounded by a broken fence, and weeds were smothering the whole yard all the way up to the doorstep. The chimney was a crumbled pile of stones at the side of the house, and if any window had glass in it at all, it was cracked.

Plus, a whole corner of the roof had already caved in.

"What are we waiting for?" said Tom. "Let's go in."

"Go in?" I said. "It doesn't seem safe to look at, let alone go into. Frankie, what do you say?"

Frankie was reading a page of the book. "It says we go in."

"Gulp," I said, gulping.

We crept to the door and looked in at a wrecked living room with a dirt floor. A sort of fireplace was on one wall and was full of fallen bricks and charred wood. In the back of the front room was a cracked staircase hanging from the upper floor at an odd angle.

"Falling down much?" I mumbled.

Tom entered first. We followed. Everywhere we turned, we got ragged cobwebs in our faces.

"Tasty," I said, wiping a thick web from my lips.

Since there was nothing much downstairs, some-body—not me—got the great idea that we should climb up those rickety stairs and poke around upstairs.

"Sort of cuts off our escape route—" said Frankie, "in case we see some of those haunted ghosts this place is supposed to be haunted with."

"Ghosts can follow a person anywhere," said Huck.

"Oh, thanks," said Frankie. "I feel so much better."

We laid our tools against the fireplace and headed one by one up the cracked and crooked stairs.

The same sort of ruin that was downstairs was upstairs, too. Broken doors, busted furniture, and dark, empty closets. Not much at all. We were about to go back down and begin digging for treasure when—

"Shhh!" said Tom, holding up his hand. "I hear someone coming!"

"It's ghosts!" said Frankie. "I knew it! Ohhhhh!"

In a flash, we were down on the floor, peering through the cracks between the planks, waiting for our hearts to stop pounding.

Two men entered the front room below us.

The first one was tall and wore a red poncho with a hood pulled over his head.

"I've seen that first one around town just after the trial," Huck whispered. "People say he's a Spaniard from Spain or someplace. The other one I don't know."

The other one was a ragged creature with a nasty face who looked as if he were a graduate of the Muff Potter School of Personal Washing. Grimy isn't the word. Dirt was cleaner than this guy.

He slung a small bag of coins onto the bare floor.

"I've thought it over," he growled in a deep voice. "It's too dangerous."

"Dangerous?" grunted the Spanish guy. "Pah!"

First of all, the Spanish guy wasn't speaking Spanish. And second of all, we had all heard that voice before.

"Oh, my gosh!" Frankie hissed. "It's—him!"

We all knew it was true. This tall Spanish guy was merely disguised as a tall Spanish guy. He was in reality a tall, stinky guy named Joe. In other words, Stinky Joe!

"We'll do the robbery, then we'll head for Texas with all the money," snarled Joe. "But first, there's some revenge that I'm planning."

"Revenge?" whispered Tom.

"On us!" whispered Huck.

"Let's bury this sack of money deep and come back after the job," said Joe. From under his poncho he pulled a knife with a blade as big as a surfboard and started hacking away at the ground near the foot of the stairs.

Suddenly, his knife struck something.

"What is it?" Dirt Guy asked.

"A box!" said Joe. "Grab those shovels and help me."

Mr. Unclean took hold of our shovels and plunged one of them deep into the ground. Joe took the other and did the same. In no time, they pulled up a strongbox. With a sharp whack of the shovel, the lid flew open.

"There's thousands of dollars here!" said Joe.

I gasped.

But not at the dollars.

There was something else in the box, too.

Frankie and I saw it at the same time and grabbed each other's arms. We stared at the box. We stared at each other, then back at the box.

"The lost page!" she whispered.

It was exactly that. The lost page of Mrs. Figglehopper's classic copy of *The Adventures of Tom Sawyer* was sitting right there with the gold and silver coins in the box. I could even see the dark scrawl of the author, Mark Twain, at the bottom of the page.

Stinky Joe shut the box with a loud clunk. "We'll take this and hide it in our secret place—you know, number two, under the cross."

We all looked at one another, puzzled.

"Number two under the cross?" I whispered. "Where is that?"

"Wait a minute," said Joe, staring at the shovels they had used to dig up the box. "Where did these tools come from?"

"Uh-oh," whispered Frankie.

Dirt Man stood up. "People brought them?"

"People . . . who might still be here?" said Joe, peering up at the ceiling. "People who might be . . . upstairs?"

I nearly had a heart attack. Forget nearly—I *did* have a heart attack!

Stinky Joe grabbed that huge battle knife of his and started up the stairs.

"We're goners!" whispered Tom. "Joe will find us and take that knife and . . ."

CR-CR-CRASH! There was a horrible crackling of rotten wood as Stinky Joe tumbled to the ground amid the ruins of the stairs.

"Yes!" I shouted. To myself.

"Ohhhh, never mind this!" groaned Joe, clambering to his feet and rubbing his shoulder. "We'll take our treasure and be gone before anyone sees us, anyhow!"

A few minutes later, the two bandits slipped out of the house and rushed away with their precious box of gold and silver.

And the even-more-precious lost page of our book.

Chapter 15

"We have to get it back!" I said to Frankie as we shot back to Aunt Polly's house.

"No kidding," she said. "If we don't get it, we might get stuck in this book forever and never make it back home. Tom, you've got to help us get that treasure box!"

But the minute we hit Aunt Polly's house, the word *treasure* faded from Tom's mind.

It was replaced by another word.

Picnic.

"I just remembered!" Tom gasped. "Becky's having her picnic today. I gotta go to that!"

Frankie gave me a look. "Oh, man, not again with the Becky business? We've got treasure to find!"

But Tom was too excited about the picnic to think about the treasure right then. "We'll go up the river to McDougal's meadow. It's the best spot for a picnic. Then we can go exploring in McDougal's cave."

"A . . . cave?" I said. "No, thanks. I don't do caves. I've already been stuck in a closet. It was like a cave in there. I didn't like it. Sorry, no caves for me."

Tom turned to me, his face alight with excitement. "McDougal's cave is deep, and filled with bats. You need candles to go in there or you might wander for days and nights and never find the way out!"

"Mmm," I said. "You do make it sound good, but no."

Shrugging, Tom left us and ran off to join the crowd gathering outside Becky's house.

Huck made a sort of grunting sound in his throat. "Picnics? Yuck. Stinky Joe used to go to a tavern in town. Maybe his secret hiding place, 'number two under the cross,' is there. We could check. And while Tom's eating pie, we'll find our treasure!"

Frankie brightened. "I like the way you think, Huck. Did I ever tell you that I think you should have your own book?"

Huck grinned. "I like that idea plenty. Now let's go find that strongbox!"

A few hours later, Huck, Frankie, and I were squirreled away in an alley in town. Night had fallen. Tom and Becky and the others had been picnicking all day, but the three of us were doing the real work of the story.

We were going to hunt down Joe's treasure!

"Joe used to hang out at the tavern across the street," said Huck, pointing to a dark building not far from where we crouched. "If he's up to his old ways, maybe we'll see him there . . . and follow him."

"Shh!" I said.

We had just enough time to slide into an alcove behind a store when two men brushed by us and onto the darkened street ahead. One of the men had something under his arm. It looked boxy and heavy.

"It's Joe all right," I gasped. "I can smell him. And he's got the box!"

Huck nodded. "Let's follow him."

We stepped out and padded behind the two men like quiet cats. They moved up the street for three blocks, then turned up a cross street to the left. Then straight ahead, then onto a path that led out of town.

"Where are they going?" asked Frankie.

We followed the men until they stopped.

"The Widow Douglas's house!" Huck whispered, pointing to a small house in the moonlit distance.

The two bad guys loomed tall on the hill over-looking the house.

Then Stinky Joe spoke. "Time for my revenge."

Huck turned to us. "Revenge? On the widow? I thought he was after *us*?"

Joe spoke again. "I never liked her. But her husband was the worst. He never treated me square. Now that I'm leaving for Texas, I've got to pay her back. I'm going to get her once and for all!"

Frankie turned. "We'd better get help. And fast!"

We stepped away as softly as we could and made our way back down the hill. We ran and ran until we reached another house.

"The old Welshman lives here!" said Huck, panting up to the front door. "We have to let him know!"

Huck banged hard on the door. An old man's head poked out a window above us. He rubbed his eyes.

"Who's there?"

"Frankie!" said Frankie.

"Who?"

"Devin!" I yelled.

"Who?"

"Huckleberry Finn!" Huck said finally.

The man snorted. "Huckleberry Finn? That isn't a name to open many doors around here. But come in and let's see what the trouble is."

The old man and his two sons let us in.

"Please don't ever tell I told you," Huck blurted out, "but the widow's been a good friend to me, and Stinky Joe is planning to hurt her!"

A minute later, the old man and his sons were up the hill near the widow's house. We tagged behind them, but then there was the sound of a gun going off. *Blam!*

"Holy cow, a battle! I'm outta here!" said Frankie.

"Me, too!" said Huck.

"Me, three!" I added.

We raced away as fast as our legs could carry us. After we ran out of steam, we stopped and listened for a while. Hearing no more shooting, Frankie and I consulted the book. After we had turned a few pages, it was the next day, so we went back to the old Welshman's place. Huck banged hard on the door once more.

The old Welshman again poked his head out of the window. "Who's there?"

"Frankie!" said Frankie.

"Who?"

"Devin!" I yelled.

"Who?"

"Huckleberry Finn!" said Huck.

The man whooped. "Huckleberry Finn! That name can open this door anytime!"

Huck smiled a surprised smile. "That's the first time I ever heard those words."

Inside, the Widow Douglas welcomed Huck with a big hug, which he tried to squeeze out of. "You saved my life!" she exclaimed.

Then the old Welshman told us how he and his sons had rescued the widow. They had fired shots at Stinky Joe and his dirty friend, but the two had escaped into the woods. "We couldn't find them anywhere."

Just then—*tap! tap!*—there was a knock on the door, and Huck nearly hit the ceiling.

"It's Stinky Joe!" he said.

"Joe probably doesn't tap on doors," said Frankie.

Suddenly, Aunt Polly rushed in. Her face was white and drawn. Her lips were pale. She was shaking.

"What is it?" the old man asked.

"It's Tom," said Aunt Polly. "And . . . Becky. They never came back from the picnic. They're lost . . . lost in McDougal's cave!"

Huck slumped down into a chair. He didn't look well. Maybe the Stinky Joe stuff had finally gotten to him. Maybe it was the news about his friend Tom. Either way, he was one sick Huck. The Widow Douglas put blankets over him and said she would take care of him.

"I'll get up a search group," said the old Welsh guy, bounding to his feet. "I only hope we can find the kids soon enough."

"I've got a faster way," I said. I grabbed the book from Frankie.

"Devin, what are you doing?"

"We need to find Tom and Becky," I said. "And we need to do it now! Hold on to your funny clothes, people—because I'm flipping ahead to the next chapter!"

I held the book in my hands and flipped one blurry page after another after another.

Suddenly—*kkkkkk!*—there was a bright flash in the room, then the room went dark, and everybody fell on everybody else in a heap of old-fashioned Mississippi River people.

The Welshman yelled out something that I hope was in Welsh. Aunt Polly's thick glasses went flying.

The air went hot, then cold. Then, amazingly, a wedge of darkness came shooting down from the ceiling, piercing the room in half like a page ripping slowly in half.

"Devin!" yelled Frankie.

But I just kept tumbling. I felt the book sliding out of my hand as I fell. The darkness widened and I slipped and—

Thud! I fell to the floor.

Only it wasn't the floor anymore.

It was cold stone. Cold, rough stone.

The cold, rough stone of . . . the cave!

Chapter 16

"Tom!"

No answer.

"Becky!"

No answer.

It was just me and lots of cold, rough stone. No old-fashioned Mississippi River people. No best pal Frankie.

And no book.

"Uh-oh," I said to no one, because no one was there.

I stood up slowly in the cave and didn't bump my head, which was a plus. But when I took my first step, my foot slid on something round and roly.

Thud-ud-ud!

"Owww!"

I slammed the stone floor hard. Groping in the dark, I found what I had tripped on.

"Yay! A candle!"

Of course, a candle by itself is just something to trip on. But a candle next to a bunch of matches? Well, I had that thing lit in no time. And in no time, I wound my way around one of the spookiest, creepiest tunnels in the world.

I remembered all over again why I hated caves so much. And I realized something else, too.

Time was flashing by. My candle was burning faster and smaller by the minute, and I was getting hungrier and more tired by the second.

It was a very weird feeling, until I figured that Frankie must be reading the book, trying to find out what would happen to Tom and Becky (and me). By the look of it, she was reading hard and fast, because sentence by sentence, time was passing quickly. I realized then that several days had passed since Tom and Becky had gotten lost. There would be little or no food left from the picnic, so the chances of finding them alive would be as slim as I bet they were getting.

"But I have to try," I said to myself, going deeper into the cave. Then I stopped.

By the glow of my candlelight I saw some black marks on the rocky wall above me.

The names "Becky" and "Tom" had been written there with candle soot.

"Hey, at least I'm going in the right direction!" I said. "Tom! Becky! Hey!"

Only echoes answered me. "Omm . . . Ecky . . . Eyyyyy . . ."

"Same to you," I muttered.

The tunnel wound this way and that, far down under the hillside. In one place I found a big cavern with lots of dripping going on from the rocks above.

A little while later, I came into another cavern that had huge bunches of bats clinging to the ceiling.

"Nice bats, stay. . . ."

I jetted out of there, hoping I wouldn't smush my nose on a stone wall, when my foot splashed into something wet. Oh, goody. I had just found myself a big underground lake. And my foot found itself wet.

"Oh, man!" I shouted.

"Oh, man, yourself!" said a familiar voice.

"Tom?" I said.

It *was* Tom. He stumbled out of the shadows, all dirty, his clothes ripped, his face dark with soot, his own candle nearly flickering out.

"Devin, is that really you?" His voice was hoarse. "You found us. We're saved! Becky, we're saved!"

Becky crept out of the shadows behind Tom. It was only then that it hit me how long the two of them had been in the cave. She was paler and dirtier than Tom, and had a strange ghostly look in her eyes.

"We're saved!" she said. Then, seeing my own look, she frowned. "We *are* saved, aren't we?"

I tried to smile. "Um . . . define 'saved' . . ."

"Oh, no!" Tom groaned.

"But you're the one who knows these caves!" I said.

"Partly," he said. "And partly not. We're in the partly-not part now."

"Oh," I said.

We started walking anyway, thinking that going in one direction was better than going in no direction. Every time we stopped to check out a new tunnel, Becky and I watched Tom's face for some kind of happy look. But he didn't have any.

"Nope," he'd mutter.

"Hey, big deal," I said. "So there aren't any big red exit signs. So what? We'll find a way out!"

But to myself I said, "Frankie, find us a way out!"

As we traveled on, the way twisted and curved in such a weird way, we couldn't tell whether we were going up or down, getting deeper into the hill, or slowly making our way out.

Tom stopped once and shouted. "Heyyyy!"

The call went echoing down the empty tunnels

and died out in the distance in a faint sound that seemed like someone laughing.

"Don't do it again, Tom," said Becky. "It's too horrid."

"Someone might hear us," said Tom.

"Might?" I repeated. "Someone better hear us! Yikes! I never thought I'd say this, but I'd rather be taking Mr. Wexler's test right now! I'm not supposed to die in this book! I mean—I'm not even in it!"

But Becky heard just one word. "Die? Oh! Die!"

She slumped down on the ground and burst into tears. "Why did we ever leave the others! Tom, we are going to die! Devin's right, isn't he!"

Tom glared at me. "Nice work, Devin."

I gulped. "Me? Right? Ha! Frankie would laugh. I myself am laughing at the silliness of it. Ha-ha. See? Don't worry, Becky. I am never right! Ask Mr. Wexler! Ask anyone!"

But Becky wasn't a dumbbell. She could see that we were in deep trouble. She buried her face on Tom's shoulder and let loose with the waterworks.

"Don't give up hope," said Tom quietly. "We'll get out of here. I know we will."

We moved on again, sort of aimlessly, but the truth was that we were getting loster and loster by the minute. Tom took Becky's candle and blew it out to save it, which we all knew was bad news, because he must have known we were in for the long haul.

After a while, Becky stopped and sat down. She was so tired, all she wanted to do was sleep. I knew it was the hunger getting to her. She was paler than pale, and her hands were shaking. It was pretty awful.

But it got even awfuler. Tom's last candle fizzled out. Everything went dark.

"Um . . . okay," I said, "what do we do now?"

No one knew. We sat silent for a while.

Finally, Tom stirred. "Wait! I have Frankie's kite string in my pocket!"

I looked at where his voice was coming from. "Good one. But we're missing a kite and we're missing a sky, remember?"

Tom shook his head. "No, I mean while Becky rests, you and me can explore these side tunnels. We'll find our way back by leaving string behind us."

"You go ahead with the kite string," said Becky. "And explore around, but just come back every little while and talk to me."

"We will," I said. "You bet. The old kite-string idea never fails."

"And promise," she said in a faint and spooky voice, "that when the time comes, you'll stay here and hold my hand until it's over."

"Over?" I said. "You talking about dying again?"

"Dying!" said Becky. "Oh! Devin's right!"

She burst into tears then, and I just about burst into tears myself, but Tom yanked my arm and said, "Devin, come on!"

Taking one end of the kite string, he tied it around a stone. Then, unwinding the rest slowly, he and I entered one of the caves. At the end of twenty feet or so, the cave ended in a jumping-off place. I got down on my knees and felt below, and then as far around the corner as I could reach.

"Anything down there?" whispered Tom.

"Maybe another tunnel, crossing below us," I said.

I stretched a little farther and at that moment, not twenty feet away, a human hand holding a candle, appeared in the tunnel below!

I got ready to shout that we were found, when instantly the hand was followed by the arm and then the body and face of . . . Stinky Joe!

I was frozen to the spot. I could not move. Stinky Joe didn't look up, or he would have seen me for sure. And seen Tom, too, for Tom had squirmed in there with me.

But Stinky Joe just strode past the opening and continued down the lower tunnel.

"L-l-let's get out of here!" I whispered.

We scuttled back a bit to where another tunnel branched off from the first, taking the string with us.

This new tunnel went farther than any one before it. The kite string unwound and unwound and finally gave out.

"That's it," I said. "Show's over. We're done. End of the road. Last stop. Roll credits. Good-bye, world!"

"Devin," said Tom.

"Good-bye, best pal, Frankie, we're through here—"

"Devin . . ."

"Good-bye, Mom, Dad, TV—"

"Devin!"

I looked at Tom. "Hey, this is my great speech. You're wrecking it. Good-bye, summer at the beach! Good-bye, trusty remote control—"

"DEV—IN!" Tom shouted.

I stopped. "What's so important?"

Tom pointed ahead to a small opening in the rocks.

And there it was, peeking through a crack in the cave wall.

The broad Mississippi River.

Just slowly rolling by.

"Yes!" I cried. "We're found! I knew we would be! Ya—hoooooo!"

Chapter 17

While Tom went back for Becky and told her the news that we were saved, I flagged down a bunch of fishermen in a small boat.

They could hardly believe my story.

"But you're five miles down the river from where the cave swallowed up those poor kids!"

"Well, the cave must have spat us out," I insisted. "Because we're here!"

When Tom and Becky came stumbling over, the fishermen fed us and brought us to town in their wagon.

You should have heard all the cheering and yelling when everyone saw us! Almost instantly, there was a big get-together at Judge Thatcher's place, with

Aunt Polly and Mrs. Thatcher and Judge Thatcher jumping up and down with joy to see us all. Huck was there, too, feeling out of place, but better after the Widow Douglas had taken care of him.

Of course, Frankie grinned the hugest grin she ever grinned when I showed up. "Good to have you back, Devin," she said.

"Hey, I almost breathed my last in that cave," I said. "But thanks for reading fast. Being alive is way better than being not."

"You *should* thank me," she said, rubbing her temples. "I have one extra-large headache brewing in here. But I guess it was sort of worth it."

Yeah, it was cool to be with my pal Frankie again.

It turns out that Tom and Becky had been in the caves for nearly a week. Judge Thatcher came over and shook my hand, thanking me for helping to find them.

"Thank you for your part in all of this, son," he said. "I'm happy to say that nobody will ever get lost in that cave again."

Tom turned suddenly. "Why, sir?" he asked.

"Because I had its big door covered in iron and triple locked. And I've got the keys!" the judge said, smiling.

Tom turned white as a sheet.

"What's the matter, boy?" the man asked.

"Judge!" I said. "Stinky Joe's in that cave!"

In a flash, a dozen boatloads of men, along with me and Tom and Frankie and Huck, shot over to the cave.

Frankie sort of summed it up for all of us when Judge Thatcher unlocked the huge cave door.

"Eeewww!"

Stinky Joe lay stretched on the ground. He was past his prime. One pulse short of being alive. In other words: he was dead.

The guy's big huge knife lay close by, its blade broken in two. The door had been chipped and hacked at, but the only real damage had been to the knife itself.

I felt sort of sorry for Stinky old Joe, because I knew how much it must have hurt to be locked in and hungry. Tom seemed torn up by it, too. But I could also tell he was relieved that Joe would threaten him and Huck no more.

Huck was sullen and sad. But not for Stinky Joe.

"That treasure is long gone," he grumbled. "With Stinky Joe dead, we have no way of finding that old number two under the cross. We all should have had it. We all should have been rich. But it slipped through our fingers."

But Tom had that old twinkle in his eye. He took us aside. "It's in the cave," he whispered.

Huck blinked at his friend. "Say that again!"

Tom smiled wide. "The treasure's in the cave!"

I jumped. "The treasure? In the box? In the cave?"

"In the cave!" said Tom. "Right near where we got out. That's where we saw Joe, and that's where the strongbox is. I'd bet my life on it!"

"I didn't see the treasure," I said. "I was there, too."

"But you aren't the hero," said Frankie, tapping the book.

As fast as you can say, "Treasure!" the four of us were squirming into the small cave opening that Tom and Becky and I had squirmed out of just a short time before.

About twenty minutes later, we were at the spot where Tom and I had seen Stinky Joe in the cave. When Tom squeezed down to the jumping-off place, he pointed his candle to something in the tunnel that Joe had walked through.

"I spotted this the first time, but it didn't mean anything to me," said Tom. "Then I got to thinking, and I remembered what it meant."

Frankie and I bent down to look at what he was pointing at. There were two cave openings cut out of the tunnel below. Above the second opening was a mark made in candle soot. It was a small, black cross.

"Number two, under the cross!" I gasped.

"Cave number two!" said Frankie. "Under the cross! That's where Joe and the dirt-faced guy must have hidden the strongbox! It's right here!"

Tom went down first, Huck second, Frankie third, and me last. We entered the second cave, and there it was—the treasure box Joe and his dirt-caked friend had found in the haunted house.

Frankie bent down to it and pried open the lid. On top of a pile of thousands of dollars was the lost page! She grabbed it and stared at it for a long time. Then, just as she opened the book to slip it back in its place, she gasped. "Oh!"

"What's the matter?" I said.

She looked up at me, then showed me her thumb. There was a dark smudge on it. "The ink from the autograph . . . I got some on me."

It was part of the *M* in the author's first name. I pressed my thumb against Frankie's and got some on me, too. "It's just what Mr. Wexler told us," I said. "The ink rubbed off on us. Cool."

Frankie slipped the page safely back into the book and closed it for a second. "Well, we found it. I guess that means we can . . . we can . . . go back now. . . . Oh, man . . ."

I felt it, too. Now that we had finally found the page, I didn't want to leave the book.

Being pals with Tom was just too much fun.

But we had to do what we had to do.

The four of us together emptied the strongbox into two sacks, and we carried the heavy treasure out of the tunnel and into the bright hot sunshine.

As we headed back to town, Frankie showed me that we only had about ten pages left in the story.

"Time for the big wrap-up," I murmured.

I was sure right about that.

Chapter 18

Before we even got to town, the old Welsh guy—whose name was really Mr. Jones—spotted us and dragged us to his house. He wouldn't say what for, except that it was "something special."

That something special turned out to be the biggest party ever for Tom and Huck. For Huck, because he had saved the Widow Douglas from Stinky Joe, and for Tom because he had saved Becky when we were lost in the cave.

The house was all decked out for a big supper, and everybody was there, whooping and hollering.

I turned to Frankie. "I like that they're being nice to Huck."

"Yeah, he deserves it," she said.

The two boys were taken upstairs and came down a little bit later all dressed in fancy new clothes. Huck looked like a cat stuck in glue, the way he squirmed and jerked around in clothes that actually fit him.

Then the Widow Douglas got up and said that she meant to give Huck a home under her roof.

"A home?" said Tom.

"A roof?" said Huck.

"Yes!" the woman prolaimed. "And Huck will be educated, too!"

"Educated?" said Tom.

"A roof?" said Huck.

"Yes!" the widow said again. "And when I can spare the money, I will start you in business with nice clothes every day!"

Tom laughed out loud. "But Huck doesn't need any money—Huck's rich!"

Everyone thought this was a joke, so they laughed pleasantly, but when Tom raced out of the house and barged back in, struggling under the weight of the treasure sacks and spilling them out on the table, no one knew what to say.

"Half's Huck's and half's mine!" proclaimed Tom.

It was cool. The look on Tom's face was all about his friend. We could tell that he didn't care so much about his own bag of money.

When everyone had stopped gasping and oohing and aahing over the money, Mr. Jones counted it.

The treasure amounted to the awesome sum of—

"Twelve thousand dollars!" the Welshman said.

Everyone gasped and oohed and aahed all over again.

"Nice ending," I said.

"Nice ending, but . . ." said Frankie, holding up the last chapter between her fingers. "It's not over yet. We still have five more pages."

"Gimme that book!" I said. "I wanna read!"

I did read. It turns out that the treasure money was put in a bank and Tom and Huck got an allowance of a dollar a day, which, let me tell you, is more than I get more than a hundred and twenty-five years later!

Judge Thatcher said that Tom could probably be a lawyer someday, or maybe a great soldier, or maybe both at the same time, since Tom could apparently do just about anything after saving Becky.

Huck, of course, tried to slink away, but the Widow Douglas really wanted to take care of him and that's what she did. Huck went to live in her house and went to school and wore clothes and everything. For three weeks, he did what he was told, then one day he turned up missing. Gone. Vanished. No Huck anywhere.

The Widow Douglas and others hunted for him all over the place. They searched high and low and even dragged the river for his body, firing the cannon the way they had done for us when we hid on the island.

But no. Huck was gone.

"I can't believe the author is going to end the story with Huck lost and maybe dead," Frankie said, when we met on the dusty main street after the last searches turned up no Huck. "I always thought Huck would have his own book one day."

I was sad, too. I liked the rumply kid. "If the story's almost over, I guess we'd better start searching for those zapper gates."

"Pssst!" We heard a sound over our shoulder and turned. There was Tom, in the shadow of a big old oak tree, crooking his finger at us, a little grin on his lips. "Up for a little adventure?" he said.

Frankie and I looked at each other.

"Well," I said. "We do have a few pages left. . . ."

She smiled. "It may be our last chance. Let's do it!"

Quietly, carefully, we followed Tom into the woods and came upon that old familiar junk heap.

And there, in the middle of it, was Huck's barrel.

Not only that, there were two feet sticking out of it.

"Huckie!" I yelped. We ran over and rolled the barrel over, and Huck came tumbling out with a laugh.

He was wearing the same old rags he had cast off to become part of society. They seemed to suit him much better.

We played for a bit, then Tom sucked in a breath and looked right at Huck. "You gotta come back to town."

"Don't talk about it, Tom," said his friend. "I've tried knives and forks and my fingers don't like them. House-living just ain't for old Huck Finn. He's too wild for it."

"Well, life after a barrel has got to feel strange," said Frankie.

"Strange!" said Huck, his eyes wide. "The widow makes me get up at the same time every morning! She makes me wash my face like it's never been washed before, and I hate a clean face—"

"Muff Potter lives!" I said.

"Plus, she won't let me sleep in the woodshed!" Huck went on. "Not to mention that them clothes are out to smother me to death! And shoes—phooey!"

"Everybody does it that way," said Tom.

"I ain't everybody," Huck growled. "I'm me."

He went on and on for about an hour, then summed up by saying, "Tom, I wouldn't be in this mess if it hadn't been for that money. So you just take my share and give me a nickel sometimes and I'll be happy. But I ain't going back. I like the river and the woods and my barrel and that's where I'm staying. You go and live that way. I can't."

Tom slumped his shoulders as if he were losing his best friend, which I guess he was. Then that twinkly look came into his eye again. "Looky here, Huck. Being rich isn't going to keep me from turning robber like we said."

Huck looked at him warily. "A robber? You sure?"

"No kidding," said Tom. "The robber life is the one for me. I'm going to have the greatest gang. But we can't let you into the gang if you aren't respectable. . . ."

Huck made a noise. "But I was a pirate."

"That's different," said Tom, nearly scoffing. "A robber is much more high-toned than a pirate is. You need to be high up in the nobility to be a proper robber."

Huck was silent for some time, lovingly touching the rim of his barrel house, mulling over what Tom had said.

"Well," he said finally, "I'll go back to the widow for a month to see if I can stand it, but you have to let me belong to the gang, Tom."

Tom leaped for joy. "We'll get the boys together and have the initiation tonight—at midnight!"

"Yay!" I said, jumping up and down. "The fun continues! I'll be Devin the Masked One, or Count Devin, the Prince of Thieves, or maybe Devin the . . ."

"Devin?" said Frankie.

I turned.

She was pointing to the woods beyond Tom and Huck.

And there it was, a blue flickering light shining through the bushes behind Huck's barrel.

The zapper gates were calling us.

Chapter 19

I was totally bummed. "Mrs. Figglehopper's zapper gates, already? Is it time to go back so soon? We're just getting started. I want to be a robber. Come to think of it, I've always wanted to be one! It's not fair."

"Hey, it's not," said Frankie. "I want to rob and pillage with Tom and Huck, too. But it seems like the end of the story. For us, at least."

We turned to the guys for maybe the last time.

". . . all the pact-making has got to be done at midnight," Tom was saying. "In the lonesomest, awfulest place you can find—"

"Maybe a haunted house?" suggested Huck.

"The hauntedest!" Tom said. "And you've got to swear on a coffin and sign it with blood—"

"More blood," said Frankie. Then she sighed. "Yeah, I guess it's time to get back to the real world."

"Back to our busy, overbooked lives," I said.

"Right," she said. "Let's zap ourselves."

I nodded. "Bye, Tom Sawyer! Bye, Huck Finn!"

Just then, a cool breeze fluttered through the hot woods. The sun was blazing overhead and streaming light down through the leafy trees, but it was comfy and nice in Huck's yard as he and Tom kept making plans.

I breathed it all in. It felt good and slow and carefree and I liked it. It was summertime for Tom and Huck, and it would always be that way in this book.

"So long, guys," Frankie said at last.

They turned and waved to us as we leaped together into the pulsing blue light of the library zapper gates.

KKKKKK! The whole world of green leaves went bright blue. Then everything went dark for a split second, and we found ourselves hurtling over each other in a mess of arms and legs and fluttering pages until—*thud!*—we hit the wall of the library workroom at the exact moment we left it.

The door squeaked, and Mrs. Figglehopper entered. "Devin . . . Frankie . . . you . . . er . . . why are you two on the floor?"

We bolted up.

"We . . . um . . . like the way the floor smells!" said Frankie.

The librarian gave us a strange look. "I see. Anyway, time's up, I'm afraid. Your test with Mr. Wexler begins in one minute. I'm sorry you didn't have much time to look at *The Adventures of Tom Sawyer*. Sometime you really ought to read it—"

"Again," I whispered to Frankie.

"Excuse me?" said Mrs. Figglehopper.

"Um . . . nothing," said Frankie.

She handed Mrs. Figglehopper the treasure. I mean, the book. "Here you go," she said.

Just before we left, Mrs. Figglehopper looked at the book, then flipped through it to the last page. She studied it for a second, glanced at us in a strange way, then smiled this tiny, odd smile to herself.

As we headed down the hall to class, Frankie turned to me. "I'm still not sure about Mrs. Figglehopper and her weird zapper gates. Do you think she knows about how they take us into books?"

I shrugged. "It is weird how she keeps them around. Maybe someday we'll find out for sure what she knows. If we ever have to read a book again."

"Something tells me we probably will," said Frankie.

When we got to class, Mr. Wexler had a huge smile on his face. "Just in time!" he boomed, his eyes blazing. "Prepare to dazzle me with your knowledge of a book I read five times when I was your age! Challenge me!"

He put the test paper down on our desks.

Frankie and I sat down and took the test.

It was awesome. I wrote more words than I thought I ever knew. Whole sentences of them. All about how the author, Mark Twain, was writing about what it was like to grow up on the banks of the Mississippi River and about friendship and the stuff friends did together. And also about summer and what it felt like a long time ago, with all the clean air and the woods and playing in the sun and not having so many worries.

I wrote about how the book was really about what it means to be a kid. The way we think and feel and how we want to do something really, really bad, then we get tired of it and move on to something else. How we're afraid sometimes, but how we get through it, anyhow.

I thought the book was also about friendship— how Tom liked Becky and Huck—and about how it makes you want to do things for your friends.

Sort of like me and Frankie, I guess.

I aced the test. Frankie did, too.

I could tell by the fish-eye look Mr. Wexler gave us when he glanced at our tests that we did really well on it.

I'm sure he couldn't figure out how we could possibly know so much about any book, let alone one of his all-time favorites.

But we'll never tell.

Dear Reader:

Did you know that Mark Twain is really the pen name of Samuel Langhorne Clemens? Well, it is. Born in 1835, Sam grew up in the little town of Hannibal, Missouri, on the banks of the Mississippi River.

As a young man, Sam was a printer's apprentice, a newspaperman, a traveler, a gold prospector, and finally a steamboat pilot on the Mississippi.

During the 1860s, he began writing travel articles and humorous stories, some of which made fun of local people. To write more freely, he chose a pen name taken from his days of piloting steamboats. "Mark twain" was the call that announced to the pilot that the river was "twain," or two fathoms deep (a fathom is six feet).

Over the next few years, Mark's reputation as a humorist grew. But it wasn't until *The Adventures of Tom Sawyer* was published in 1876 that he was recognized as one of America's greatest writers for the way he captured how children really feel and think and talk.

How did he do it? He went back to his own boyhood.

"Most of the adventures recorded in this book really occurred," Twain says in a preface. "Huck Finn is drawn from life; Tom Sawyer, also, but not from an individual; he is a combination of the characteristics of three boys whom I knew." We know, however, that Twain himself was the most important model for Tom.

And Frankie will like that Huck did indeed get his own book. *The Adventures of Huckleberry Finn* is felt by many to be Twain's greatest work.

During his lifetime, Twain was considered America's finest comic writer. He is still revered today for the same reason. By the time he died in 1910, he had written many books, but his most famous will always be the adventures of Tom and Huck on the banks of the Mississippi.

I must stop now. I hear a noise in the workroom.

Until then, toodle-oo! See you where the books are!

I. M. Figglehopper

#3: What a Trip!
(*Around the World in Eighty Days*)

Chapter 1

"Everyone ready for our field trip?" my English teacher, Mr. Wexler, chirped. "All right, then. Let's go!"

"This is a field trip?" a voice hissed in my ear. "I don't call this a trip. Devin, do you?"

I'm Devin Bundy. The person hissing in my ear was my-very-best-friend-despite-the-fact-that-she's-a-girl, Frankie Lang. We're in the sixth grade at Palmdale Middle School, and at the moment, we were following Mr. Wexler and the rest of our class on a field trip.

Down the hall and around the corner.

To the school library.

"I think this is definitely stretching the definition of field trip," I replied to Frankie as we tramped past the main office. "I see no fields, because we are totally

1

inside. And I usually reserve the word 'trip' for something that involves a bus with a bathroom. But then, I didn't hear Mr. Wexler even talking about a trip because I was working on another project."

Frankie frowned at me. "What other project?"

"A dream I was having. I dreamt that I was sleeping in class and having a dream about sleeping in class."

She nodded. "Devin, you've had that dream before."

"It's one of my favorites," I said.

Now, there's something you need to know about Frankie and me. People say that the only way to succeed in life is to develop your talents. So we have.

Frankie is really amazing at staring into space.

My own specialty is dozing in class.

Hey, it's what we do well.

What we don't do well is read. We test pretty low on the whole book-reading thing. Of course, Mr. Wexler wants to help us do better. He's sure we have great potential.

"Everyone—here we are!" Mr. Wexler said excitedly as we reached the library entrance.

Frankie was so disappointed, her hair drooped.

"I bet Mrs. Figglehopper is behind this whole field trip thing," she said. "She'll probably pop out from behind a book and make us read something!"

Mrs. Figglehopper is the not-too-ordinary librarian of Palmdale Middle School. She always wears long, flowery dresses. Her gray hair is tied up in a tight knob at the back of her head. And she's severely nutty about old books. You know the kind of books I mean? People call them classics.

Mrs. Figglehopper and Mr. Wexler were like the one-two punch of reading. He assigned fat old books, and her library had loads of copies of them.

But that wasn't the only thing about our teacher and librarian. Because of stuff we've done, and some stuff we haven't done, Mr. Wexler has sentenced us to work in Mrs. Figglehopper's library workroom a couple of times.

And let me tell you something. The weirdest things happen in that library workroom.

As we stood outside the library, Frankie and I glanced at each other. I could tell from the look in her eye that we were both remembering some of those weird things.

"Zapper gates," whispered Frankie.

"Zapper gates," I whispered back to her.

The zapper gates are what Mrs. Figglehopper calls an old set of security gates that she keeps in the workroom. They're the kind of gates that are supposed to *zzztzzt!* when you take a book through them that hasn't been checked out right.

The librarian told us, like, a thousand times that those gates were broken and that someday she'll get them repaired to work right again.

Except that the gates weren't exactly broken.

Frankie and I found out that those gates can sizzle and fizzle and spark and flicker and drop you right into a book.

Yes! Into a book! Right there with all the characters and places and story and everything!

The first time it happened, Frankie and I were fighting over a book. It fell through the gates, light exploded everywhere, and the wall behind the gates cracked open.

When we went through, we ended up right smack at the beginning of the book. Our only way home was to follow the characters all the way to the end of the story.

We almost didn't believe it had actually happened. Except that we got our best grades ever when we got tested on the books we fell into. And you can't take our grades away. They're part of our permanent record.

Mr. Wexler snapped his fingers and said, "Enter!" and we pushed through the library's double doors into the main room. It was filled with study carrels and tables and lots and lots of bookshelves, each one jammed with—guess what?—books.

I felt an uncontrollable urge to yawn.

"Devin," said Mr. Wexler, "if you can get your head out of that *fog* you're in, you might learn something fun!"

I stifled the yawn, but I knew it would come back.

"Good," said our teacher. "Mrs. Figglehopper has prepared for us a special display of beautiful books from many different countries around the world. England, India, China, Japan, France . . . ah!"

Just as my yawn made a return visit, Mr. Wexler's eyes lit up with excitement. He scampered over to a small display in the center of the room.

On the display were two things: a book and a watch. The book had a crusty green cover and looked old. The watch was one of those ancient pocket types that people used to have before they invented wrists or something. Right now, the top of the watch was flipped open, but the watch wasn't ticking.

"Class, this great classic adventure is one of the centerpieces of the display," Mr. Wexler said, picking up the book carefully. "It is called *Around the World in Eighty Days*. It's a fabulous story published in 1873 by the French author Jules Verne. Few of us get to go on a journey around the world, but we can get a sense of what it's like by reading this classic book."

"Why is there a watch on display, too?" I asked.

"Good question," said Mr. Wexler. "To find out the answer, all you have to do is . . ."

5

"What?" said Frankie.

"Read the book!"

"Not fair," I grumbled.

Mr. Wexler put the book down. "Now, please follow me. We only have about an hour and twenty minutes—oh! That's funny! Eighty minutes. Let's take our tour around the world of books in eighty minutes! Eighty days, eighty minutes? Get it?"

We got it. It wasn't all that amazing.

"And . . . here we go!" he said. He marched off to the first display table. The other kids followed him.

The pain was too much for my head. I turned to my friend. "Eighty whole minutes? I can't do booky things for that long. My head starts to explode. I say we head straight for the food."

"What food?" asked Frankie.

I pointed to a table outside the workroom in the corner. On it was a big pink box. "Doughnuts, my friend, doughnuts. My nose can spot them a mile away."

Frankie grinned, glanced at Mr. Wexler, then stepped slyly up to the book display. "Devin, I'll pretend to examine this old busted watch while you pretend to read this old book. With Mr. Wexler thinking we're working, we'll take our own little field trip to Doughnutville."

"Frankie, I love how you think. Let's do it!"

I picked up the book and held it as if I were reading; Frankie took the watch and pretended to be amazed at the cool oldness of it. We headed for the pink box.

When we got near, we heard low voices coming from the workroom. Peeking in, we saw Mrs. Figglehopper and a guy in blue overalls standing in front of the zapper gates.

"What's going on?" Frankie asked.

"Mrs. F and some work guy," I whispered.

Then, to our shocked eyeballs, the work guy pulled a screwdriver from his tool belt, knelt down, and began to take the zapper gates apart!